THE LAST CHANCE ROAD TRIP

A SWEET, SMALL TOWN ROMCOM NOVELLA

SARA JANE WOODLEY

Val & Ethan art by
VECTORSMARKET

 ELEVENTH AVENUE
PUBLISHING

1

VAL

I made a mistake.

A colossally huge, bonkers mistake. At some point in my life, I must've crossed a black cat, or accidentally broken a mirror, or stepped on a magical bug that cursed me.

It's the only possible explanation for why I'm here today, at twenty-one years old.

Stuck in a tree.

Yet, regardless of how I got here, none of that changes my reality. Which is this: I, Valentina Brinn Reyes-Murphy, a grown woman with a respectable, brand-spanking-new job at our town's Inn, am clinging onto a branch in an ancient relic of a childhood treehouse. Complete with ripped pants.

Didn't I tell you? Bonkers. But at least it can't get any worse.

Or so I believed until the guy I grew up with, the guy I dated for two world-changing months before he broke my heart appears right below me.

He doesn't see me right away, and I pray to every single deity, ruler of the universe, and magical bug for it to stay that way. The last thing I need is for Ethan Holmes to see

1

me like this—hanging onto a tree branch for dear life with my pink good-luck granny-panties on full display.

And to think that today started off so well...

I woke up this morning buzzing with nervous excitement for my first day working as a receptionist at the Brookrose Inn. I got my degree in Travel and Tourism this past spring and worked all summer in a restaurant, waiting for *this* moment. My chance to finally move forward from the past and be my "highest self." To find out exactly who I am since my breakup this past February.

Yes, this girl's had two significant relationships end within the past four years. Which seems high for my age. Mom says that I have an old soul, but shouldn't I be out sowing corn, or whatever the expression is?

I digress. I had breakfast and was out the door with plenty of time to get to the Inn. But as I walked, I found my legs taking me elsewhere. Taking me here.

To the treehouse.

I don't often come here, but today, it felt right. Maybe I was nostalgic or something, remembering the happy days of my childhood. Back before Ethan left for Montana and I began dating Randal. That was his name, by the way—the guy I dated for three and a quarter years.

Anyway, I got to the treehouse, pulled down the old, frayed rope ladder, and climbed up through the trapdoor in the floor. I didn't see the branch until it scraped along my upper thigh. I felt the fall breeze on my behind and knew the damage had been done.

So while already planning a quick detour back to my house to change my pants—but not wanting to give up on my nostalgia-fueled mission quite yet—I sat on the creaky floor and took a couple deep breaths. Noticed the old, peeling glow-in-the-dark stars, the fairy lights with bulbs that don't work anymore. I grimaced at the small, dark hole in the corner wall. The one that looked like the perfect hiding spot for all kinds of critters and bugs.

Maybe even... *spiders.*

And that's where I was, sitting cross-legged and grimacing at the forbidding, spider-infested (probably) hole when Ethan Holmes appeared out of nowhere and took up residence directly below me.

Like, not two feet away.

I'd recognize that shaggy mahogany-brown hair anywhere. Not to mention his unmistakable height and those broad shoulders—the combination of which always made me feel like I was a cute, dainty fairy whenever I was with him. A rare occurrence for me given that these hips definitely don't fall anywhere near the "Tinkerbell" category.

Ethan peers up at the treehouse, and I press myself against the wall. I hold my breath.

Please don't come up here!

And also, why are you here?!

Since moving away right before our senior year, Ethan's been back to Mirror Valley a few times, and I've gone to great lengths to avoid him every time he's come to town. I steered clear of the gym he used to go to, and the bookstore he once loved. I made sure not to drop by the Valley Roast—my favorite coffee shop—or eat at the restaurants in town. One Christmas, he suddenly came around a corner and I ducked behind a bush so fast, I pulled my hamstring. Another time, I crab-walked behind some unsuspecting woman's stroller until he passed me by.

But it was all worth it. Because he never saw me.

I may have all the grace of an overexcited corgi, but I can move like a wily cat when I need to.

Of course, I know why Ethan's back in Mirror Valley this time around... his granddad Alfie passed away last

3

week. It wasn't a surprise—he'd been sick for a long time. I used to visit him all the time. Pops, as we called him, was a huge part of my childhood, too.

I should've expected to see Ethan again, but I couldn't have done anything to prepare for *this* particular scenario.

All of a sudden, Ethan lifts his head towards me.

I squeeze my eyes shut as my heart skips a long beat. *No, no, no!*

Silence.

I carefully open one eye, see that Ethan is looking away, towards the massive tree trunk.

Phew.

While he's otherwise occupied, I take my chance to assess him. For all the work I've done avoiding him over the years, I haven't actually, properly *looked* at him. My perch affords me a pretty unobstructed view for creeping.

Ethan looks... the same. But different. Like someone took the boy I grew up with and added angles and facial hair and a sort of unaffected confidence you only get when you've graduated at the top of your class in culinary school (I assume). His jawline is sharper than it used to be—in fact, he's lost a lot of his chubby-cheeked baby face. Maybe it's the stubble though, which is longer and more stubbly than I would've expected for him. A faint tan line skates along the edges of his cheekbones. Clearly, it was a sunny summer wherever he was. Montana, still?

My eyes follow the line of his nose as he stares at the gargantuan trunk. Growing up, his nose was too big for his face, but he certainly grew into it. Really well, I might add. It's a strong nose, the kind of nose you see on those statues of naked Greek gods.

Yeah. That's *what matters right now, Val.*

He runs his hand along the bark of the tree, then, to my

surprise, he places his fingers in the wide, almost perfectly rectangular gash in the trunk.

He remembers.

We used to call that hole the "letter box," and we'd leave each other notes in there. Though he'd leave my notes hanging out a little so I didn't have to risk any encounters with lurking spiders.

That all feels like a lifetime ago.

He's fiddling with something, but I can't see what it is. I lean further out, trying to see what he's doing. *Why is he...?*

At that moment, there's a brush along my hand.

A chill rockets down my spine.

A horrifically huge, fuzzy *thing* is scuttling across my fingers.

"ARGH!!!!" I shriek, shaking my hands out. It's only then that I realize the fuzz was actually a large piece of dark lint from an old blanket and not a spider.

But it's too late, because I've lost my balance.

And then, I'm falling. Flopping unceremoniously out of the treehouse and towards the ground.

I'm still screaming, limbs flailing, as I succumb to gravity.

I clench my eyes shut, waiting for impact.

It doesn't come. Instead, I'm caught—that is the literally the only way to describe it. I'm caught like my body's an old rug: an arm below my knees, an arm cradling under my back.

My hands instinctively grasp for the catcher's shoulders. My body's tensed from the anticipation of pain, and my scream catches in my throat. I open my eyes, find myself staring into lazy, dark ones I'd recognize anywhere.

"Hey, Teeny," Ethan drawls in his smooth, pepper-grinder voice. "Spying on me again?"

2

VAL

Four Years ago

"Val, what's taking so long?" Mom hollers from the bottom of the stairs. "Your sisters are waiting in the car. We're going to be late!"

"One sec!" I call back, then remove my hand from over Ethan's mouth. He laughs quietly and takes my hand in his, but my eyes are wide with concern. "What are you going to do?" I whisper.

Ethan shrugs, runs his hand across the brand-new stubble on his jawline. I won't say that I love his face more now because I don't think that's possible, but I'm certainly appreciating the new look. It makes him seem more grown up. Mature. "Don't worry about me, I'll sneak out your window. It's not like I've never done it before."

"Make sure you don't fall into Mom's carrot patch. Last time, I panicked and told her that there was a raccoon fight below my window."

"First rule of raccoon fight club..." Ethan deadpans. Then he shrugs, lips quirked in a half-smile. "I don't think she'd mind if she knew it was me."

"You don't know how proud she is of her carrots."

"How about I make up for it by mediating the next time Carmen and Alicia get into it?"

"Nothing you've done could be bad enough to warrant refereeing my sisters' fights as a punishment." I bite my lip to hide a smile. "But seriously, I don't think Mom would be happy to hear that you've been sneaking into my room at night. Things are... different now."

"Not *that* different." Ethan's deep brown eyes sparkle as they meet mine and the butterflies that have taken up residence in my stomach fly free once again. "We had a sleepover. Like we've done since we were five."

I fiddle with the bottom of my pajama top—a huge, faded blue shirt with the Top Gun logo splashed across the front. It used to be Ethan's, but I have full custody now. "Well, given that you're my boyfriend now, Mom might not necessarily believe us."

"Why wouldn't she?" He looks at me oh-so-innocently. "Last I checked, she still loves me."

"Only because you bribe her with freshly-made treats whenever you come over."

"Love through bribery is still love."

I snort with laughter and Ethan silences me with a kiss.

Yes, he spent the night last night. And no, nothing *happened*. Ethan is and has always been my favorite sleepover buddy. Maybe because his arms fit so perfectly around me, or he heats up like a furnace in his sleep and the coziest spot in the world is cuddled up next to him.

On Ethan's part, I think he's also happy not to spend the nights alone. His mom's been stuck working the night shift at the hospital for months. She hates being away from him in the evenings, but she's had a tough time finding a security job with daytime hours here in Mirror Valley.

Not that I'm complaining. Ethan and I used to have

sleepovers all the time, but when we began dating at the start of the summer, our parents seemed less than thrilled with the idea of us having any more. We stopped for a couple weeks, followed their rules. But I missed him, and he missed me, so now, we keep it a secret. My one and only teenage rebellion.

I still can't believe this is happening. I've had a crush on Ethan for as long as I can remember, and when he kissed me on the last day of junior year, I almost fainted with happiness like the heroines in my favorite regency romance novels.

Just give me a lounger and one of those rigid corsets, and I would've collapsed like Lady Mirror...shire.

"You getting ready or what?" Ethan whispers, tickling me in the side. "Your mom's going to get suspicious."

"I can't exactly change while you're lurking."

"I'm not lurking. I'm an innocent bystander."

I sigh, putting on the annoyed face I reserve for him. "Okay, *innocent bystander*, you stand in the corner facing the wall, and I'll change into my dress. And don't even *think* about spying on me."

"What? I am a perfect gentleman. In fact..." He holds out a hand, puts on a terrible British accent. "You dare assume me to be the most unmitigated and comprehensive a—"

I smack a hand over his mouth again, holding back a giggle. We watched *Pride and Prejudice* last night, buried beneath my covers with the volume on one bar so my family wouldn't hear. Honestly, I thought Ethan slept through the whole thing.

"You fancy yourself as Mr. Bingley, then?" I ask, testing him.

"More like Mr. Darcy."

I roll my eyes, then signal for him to turn around. Ethan

covers his face, but peeks through his fingers to give me a final once-over. I gesture for him to turn away again, and he sighs dramatically before turning towards the wall.

I watch his back for a few moments. Not because I think he'd break his promise (he wouldn't) but because, for the thousandth time this summer, I'm overcome with happiness.

I always believed that Ethan Holmes was my soulmate. Even before I knew that he felt the same way I did—when I was lost in the melodramatic throes of seemingly-unrequited love—I knew that we were meant to be in each other's lives. Even if we were just friends.

But we've been dating for two months now, and I can't believe how hard and fast I've fallen for him. And with every loaded look, every sweet kiss, every tender inside joke, I know he's fallen just as hard for me. We're going into our senior year, and I can already see our lives together—walking to class hand in hand, dancing at our senior prom... Ethan will go to culinary school in Denver, and I'll study either tourism or veterinary medicine, hopefully close by. Regardless of where we go to school though, it won't keep us apart.

Ethan is like an arm to me. A sweet, handsome, totally loveable arm.

Now he shifts, still facing the wall. "I don't hear anything. You getting changed?"

My throat is a little thick and I clear it before I answer, hoping I sound normal. "Almost ready."

Ugh. So much for normal. My voice sounded like when I watched *The Notebook* (AKA when the deluge lasted for hours).

As expected, Ethan turns to face me, concern etched across his features. He strides towards me. "Teeny, you okay?"

I shake my head. "I'm fine, I'm fine. Sorry. I'm just... happy."

Ethan's brow unfurrows and his eyes search mine. Deep brown eyes with speckles of silver that I could never, ever get tired of looking at. His lips tip up into a lopsided smile. "Happily... staring at my butt?"

My mouth drops open. "Was not!"

"Was too!" He chuckles, then hugs me tighter. "But it's okay. I like when you spy on me."

I purse my lips, then step back and signal for him to turn around. "Go on, I have to get changed. All your dilly-dallying is making me late."

3

ETHAN

My grandma used to say that it was a sign of luck if things fell into your lap.

I don't think having your ex-girlfriend literally fall on top of you was quite what she had in mind.

"Long time, no see," I say as Val continues to stare at me. Her mouth is a perfect oval, her amber eyes glittering pools of shock. I start to wonder if I've missed something—maybe I have something on my face. A spider?

I can't check given that my arms are otherwise occupied. But knowing Val—well, how she used to be—she'd be screaming and whacking me in the face if that was the case.

So, I think I'm safe.

Finally, she blinks, seems to come to her senses.

"Ethan!" she shouts. "You look well!"

"That was a close one. You okay?"

"Of course! I'm fine!"

She starts wriggling around and it occurs to me that I probably should've set her down ages ago. I place her on the ground and she stands stiffly, careful not to turn her back on me. I run my fingers across my jaw, feeling a little awkward.

And *this* is awkward.

Val and I haven't been alone together for almost exactly four years. You'd remember the day you made a decision that permanently altered your life path, too. A decision that you've thought about so often, it's started to feel like one of those fever dreams where bears or giant popsicles are chasing you…

I'm getting off track. I've seen Val from a distance when I visited Mirror Valley, caught her skulking behind trees and bushes and even a stroller once. I reached out to her multiple times, tried to bridge the gap, but she never responded. So I did my part to steer clear of her, too. We might've been close in the past, but things are different now.

Val and I are basically a walking, talking billboard example of the ways dating a childhood friend could go horribly wrong.

I never, ever thought that I'd regret dating Val, but I do.

If we hadn't dated, I might not have lost her.

I glance down her body and register her gray dress pants, the white shirt beneath a nice blazer. "You're dressed awfully nice for a visit to the treehouse."

Val's cheeks turn pink. "I'm on my way to work."

"Really? Where are you working?"

"The Brookrose." Her lips quirk up. "Today's my first day."

I nod, feeling a burst of pride for her. "That's awesome, Teeny. So you decided to study tourism."

Val freezes for a half second and I do, too. Was that a weird thing to say? Back when we were dating, Val wasn't sure what she wanted to study. We used to joke about whether we'd end up working in similar career paths. "Two peas in a pot" was what Val (incorrectly) called it. Her misremembered expressions, said with so much sincerity, used to crack me up.

Then again, no one has ever made me laugh like Val has.

But that's all in the past now.

"Anyway." I clear my throat, my voice robotic. "What were you doing in the treehouse?"

Val looks at the house, grimaces like she did at the kid who peed in the ball pit when we were six (true story). "Oh, you know... First day jitters weren't enough. Thought I'd risk my life on top of it all."

"You always did know how to make an entrance."

Her grimace deepens, but this time, it's directed at me. "Yeah, well... I was taking a breather up there, and then I wanted to come down, but I saw you and..."

"You thought the best way to alert me to your presence was to scream and fall on me?"

A small smile tugs at her lips. "Exactly. Surprised?"

"You got me."

Val giggles—a short, little laugh—and she looks back at the treehouse. I scan her side profile; I haven't seen her up close like this in so long. Mascara lines her lashes, and her round cheeks are the same soft pink as strawberry ice cream.

The makeup enhances her features, but what I always loved most about Val were the things she used to say she hated—the slightly crooked front tooth in her smile, the birthmark on her collarbone, her curly brown hair... today tamed into a ponytail. In school, she used to straighten it with that hot iron thing. Flatten it to within an inch of its life. I still don't understand why basically burning your hair off was a trend, but it made her happy, so it made me happy.

I did love its natural state, though—made her look like one of those fairies in a storybook. Especially with her tiny nose and sparkling amber eyes.

She shakes her head, and I look away just as she turns to

me. "I should get going." She sighs. "New job to work, guests to check in."

"Right. Of course." I step out of the way.

But Val doesn't walk past me. Instead, she stands for a moment, a frown puckering her brow.

Then, for some inexplicable reason, she whips off her blazer and ties it around her waist. She shoots me a bright smile, and jogs off down the road. She doesn't look back as she disappears around the corner, leaving me alone in front of our treehouse with the rope ladder at my feet. In Val's tumble, it came down with her.

I'll have to fix that. And be sure to keep my distance. After everything that's happened between Val and me, the least I can do is give her the space she clearly wants.

I stick my hand in the letter box one final time before I continue on to the will reading.

4

ETHAN

Four Years Ago

I manage to make it out of Val's room, down the trellis, and through the front yard without squashing Mrs. Reyes-Murphy's thriving carrot patch. Val was right—her mom is crazy proud of her carrots. As she should be; home-grown veggies are the best.

I intend to incorporate that into my cheffing at culinary school in Denver. It's a short drive from Mirror Valley so I can stay close to my mom, grandparents, and of course, Val.

I'm not exactly thrilled about this sneaking around Val and I are doing these days. It's difficult given the years that I had to hide what I was feeling for her. Now that we're finally together, I don't want to have to hide it anymore.

Val is my oldest friend, the girl I grew up with, my first crush. If this was one of Val's cheesy movies, she's the girl next door. Yeah, I tried to branch out, date other girls in my freshman and sophomore years, but I always came back to her. Always had her in the front of my mind.

So on the last day of junior year, while the school was celebrating the start of summer, I took Val's hand. I wasn't thinking of our friendship, wasn't thinking of any potential consequences. I turned her to face me, looked deep into her eyes, and we both went quiet. I can't really explain it, but this intensity sparked between us. An abrupt change, like a lightswitch turning on.

I think I made the first move, leaned in. Val met me halfway.

We've been inseparable—even more inseparable—ever since.

This morning, Val's off to church with her family, but we'll get together later. I have a surprise for her. She's usually the one surprising me, but I'm pretty sure she won't see this one coming.

I start to walk towards my house, then detour towards town instead. Pops and Nana aren't morning people, so by the time they wake up and get to my room to see that I'm not there, they'll probably assume that I went to the Valley Roast for coffees.

My walk takes me right past the park where Val and I have our treehouse. It feels odd to say that my favorite place in the world is up a tree, but here we are. Pops and I built it a couple years ago, and it's sort of a hideaway now for Val and me.

As I'm walking by, I spot a figure standing at the base of the tree. A figure wearing familiar khaki shorts, a blue polo, and sensible sneakers.

"Pops?" I call.

He whirls around to face me. "Ethan! There you are."

I jog over to him and he claps me on the shoulder, smiling wide. His face is tanned—that nice level of weathered that looks like he just came in from a hard day's work on a fishing boat. Though, by "hard day's work," it's more likely that he spent hours lazing in the sun with his hat over his eyes and a fishing rod propped beneath his boot while chatting with his friend Ray.

"You're up early this morning," I say.

"As are you." His watery blue eyes sparkle. The ever-growing bald patch on the top of his head shines bright in the morning sun. "What're you doing wandering around at this hour?"

Okay, Ethan. Play it cool...

"Coffee!" I burst out.

Nailed it.

Pops raises a brow and I keep my expression carefully neutral even as a cool feeling licks at my stomach.

One of Pops's all-time favorite pastimes is solving mysteries. He's obsessed with treasure hunts and secret missions; the kinds of adventures that belong in spy novels or that Nic Cage movie with the Declaration of Independence. Seriously. When that movie came out, Nana joked that he wasn't even that excited on their wedding day.

A statement which I fully doubt, by the way. My grandparents have been married for thirty-five years and are still so in love, it's nauseating. In a nice way. For most people.

The thing is, Pops is absurdly proud of our last name—"Holmes." If he had the chance, he'd try to convince you we were somehow related to Conan Doyle's world-famous character. It actually took three sit-down discussions with Mrs. Perez to convince *me* that no, I was not related to a highly-intelligent yet fictional Sherlock.

Which is why his alert gaze is making me more than a little uneasy...

"Going to get us some coffees from the Roast," I repeat with a touch more conviction.

"Is that so?" Pops's gaze drops down my body and I suddenly remember that I'm wearing the same shirt I was wearing yesterday. And my stubble is probably less five-o-clock shadow and more seven-in-the-morning messy.

That'll teach me to get excited when my beard stopped growing in so patchy.

"Yes," I say, but it comes out sounding more like a question. I clear my throat. "I decided to take a detour to the treehouse first."

Pops's eyes clear. "I see. Well, I appreciate that, son. I slept like the dead last night, and could really use a good coffee. How'd you sleep?"

I smile, relieved that we've moved past the interrogation. "Really well, thanks."

"Glad to hear it. And how about Val?"

My mouth dries. Pops's question seems so innocent, but I could swear his eyes show a glimmer of mischief.

Oh, for the love... Does he know?

I clear my throat again. "Uh, probably okay? She's at church this morning, so we'll see each other later."

"Good. She's such a sweet girl. I'm glad you two finally got together. Ray and I used to talk about it all the time."

I roll my eyes. "I swear you two run the Mirror Valley rumor mill."

"Someone's got to," Pops harrumphs. Then, his face brightens and he leans in. "Are you excited for the *big* surprise tonight?"

My stomach swirls with both excitement and nerves. "I am. I hope it's not too much."

"She'll love it." He claps me on the shoulder again. "Now let's get going. Best we grab those coffees and get home before Nana's awake. Give you a chance to change out of yesterday's clothes."

With that, Pops strolls off, whistling away like he hadn't just caught me smack-dab in the middle of a bald-faced lie.

18

5

VAL

"Oh, my gosh. Oh, my giddy gosh," I mutter over and over as I hightail it to the Brookrose.

By the time I left Ethan at the treehouse, standing open-mouthed and reeling—or so I imagined—I was out of time. I stood at a literal crossroads, trying to decide if I should zip home to change my pants and be late for work, or if I should go to work with my stupid blazer tied around my waist like a six-year-old on a water break from Pee Wee soccer.

In the end, I decided that the waist-blazer was the better choice. So here I am, running for my life in the suit that I've had stowed away for this exact day—a charcoal gray pantsuit with a cream blouse. My hair is neat and gathered back into a ponytail, and I'm wearing *just* the right amount of makeup, according to my sisters.

I look prim and professional. I look like the New Val (™ pending). Or I did until the treehouse incident (RIP pants).

And that isn't even the most embarrassing part of that incident.

How stupid I must've looked, gawking at Ethan for a hundred years before finally scrambling out of his arms. I also wasn't the only one impacted by my fall—I managed to bring the rope ladder down with me.

The rope ladder. Which had been attached to the wood with *actual nails*.

The mere thought makes my body heat like it's being raked over coals of humiliation.

But what sort of crazy twist of fate has me falling out of a treehouse and into the arms of my ex-boyfriend? An ex-boyfriend I haven't spoken to, by the way, since we broke up. If this was a movie or a regency romance novel, it'd be a quirky re-meet-cute. But this is not a movie, it's my life.

A veritable comedy of errors over here.

No, Val. Don't go there. I banish the self-doubt, resolve to hold my head high. These days, I'm all about the confident, sure-of-herself New Val.

New Val who is *not* late for her first day of work.

"I'm here!" I cry as I race into the lobby of the Brookrose.

Ivy Brooks is bent over the front desk and she looks up in surprise, her glasses perched on her nose. Her eyebrows raise as she smiles at me. "What's the rush, Val? You're right on time."

Panting, I check the clock on the wall.

Phew. Five minutes early, even.

I take a moment to gather myself, then stride towards the desk, channeling every ounce of confidence I have (which is a challenge given the whole sweating, panting, waist-blazer situation).

"Morning, Ivy. How was your weekend?" My voice is calm and professional. Almost like I practiced in front of the mirror for a few hours last night. Which absolutely did not happen...

I've just been so excited to start this new job, and I'm

determined to make a great first impression. This receptionist role feels like the perfect step forward.

Plus, I did my research—small-town-gossip-mill research, I mean. I don't know Ivy well given that she's a couple years older than me, but I have a feeling we'll get along well. She has a reputation for being bright and ambitious, and people say she's very kind... except to one of her brother's friends that she had a huge feud with in school. I never got the full story around that though.

Ivy turns back to the reservation book. "I didn't do much, mostly worked all weekend. My grandparents and I are excited to have you on board."

"Me too!" My voice is squeaky and eager.

Calm down. You're still walking around with a hole in your pants.

Ivy's brow suddenly wrinkles and her mouth twists. "Everything okay?"

"Oh, yeah," I say quickly. "Why?"

Her eyes drop down to my waist level. "Because you're... well, you're..."

All at once, I realize that, while I was thinking about the hole in my pants, I was actually touching where the hole *would* be beneath the blazer.

AKA it looks like I've been standing here rubbing my butt.

I drop my hands immediately. "My pants ripped!" I basically shout.

Ivy looks understandably shocked for a fraction of a second and I wonder whether I've lost my job within the first few seconds of starting. How on earth am I going to explain this to Carmen after all the time she put in helping me with my makeup?

But then, Ivy snorts. Lets out a loud laugh. "Been there. And you're in luck, I think I have a spare skirt here somewhere. I went to the gym at lunch a couple days ago and brought a change of clothes. It's a little habit I'm trying to get into. See?"

She proudly holds up a forest green athletic shirt and a pair of black leggings. I offer a smile, cheeks still flaming, but before I can say anything, she dives back behind the front desk.

When she emerges again, she's holding a piece of black fabric. "Skirt to the rescue!"

"Are you sure?" I shift on my feet.

"Yes. Please. I know how nerve wracking your first day at a new job can be. Especially when things aren't exactly going according to plan."

I smile gratefully and run to get changed, my cheeks finally starting to cool down. I scramble out of my pants, and wince when I see the ginormous tear across the posterior.

It occurs to me that I might not have been so deathly embarrassed earlier had it been anyone but Ethan. Seriously, though, why did he have to look like *that*? It's almost comical how attractive he is now. Even up close, the only flaw is the lone scar on his nose. And his slightly lopsided smirk when he called me "Teeny."

I still don't know why he gave me that nickname. It certainly can't have anything to do with my curves, which I've been trying hard to embrace lately.

This might be the sole thing I have in common with muscly club bouncers called "Tiny."

As I slip back into my blazer, Ethan's familiar, warm, almost firewood-y scent hits me. All of a sudden, I'm thinking of the cozy nights we spent together, wrapped up in blankets and talking for hours. Even now, the scent makes my head spin.

It's enough to make a girl almost forget our entire history together.

Almost.

Because I haven't forgotten what happened, and the reminder is like being dunked into a bucket of ice water.

I head back to the front desk, bow my head shyly. "Thanks again, Ivy."

"Anytime. I keep telling myself that I need to bring an extra suit to work. Maybe this'll kick my butt into gear and make me do it."

"Yeah, my ex was all about having a change of clothes 'just in case,'" I say dryly. "You should've seen how many bags he'd bring on vacation, it was—" I stop myself, smile faltering. I shouldn't be talking about Randal. Not when I'm so focused on moving forward. "Sorry, I shouldn't have said that."

"It's okay," Ivy says, kindly overlooking my useless contribution. "Was it recent?"

"A few months back. But it was for the best, honestly. No sense talking about it."

Ivy suppresses a yawn. "Well, no one else is checking out today and we're only doing training for the next few hours. Plus, I do enjoy some idle gossip to start the morning, sooooo... spill."

She waggles her eyebrows and I chuckle, getting comfortable behind the front desk. I'm surprised how at ease I feel given that this is my first day of work. "Well, we were together for three years, but he broke up with me this past Valentine's Day."

The smile falls off Ivy's face. "He didn't."

"He did." I nod, mouth turned down. "Breaking up with a girl called Valentina on Valentine's Day. He thought there was some tragic irony to it."

"What on earth does *that* mean?"

"He... had a strange sense of humor."

"I'll say. You're better off without him, in my opinion. Nobody deserves to be treated like that by someone they thought they could trust. I remember, my brother's friend, James—" She cuts herself off. Shakes her head with a grimace. This must be the guy she had a feud with, but I don't feel I know her well enough yet to ask more about it. "Doesn't matter. Where can I find this guy? I'll give him a piece of my mind."

"He doesn't live in Mirror Valley anymore. But really, it's fine. We'd been growing apart for a long while, and we both saw it coming. We weren't meant to be."

"I get it, but even so, breakups are the *worst*..." Ivy pauses. "I assume. I haven't actually dated all that much since starting to work here. The Brookrose keeps me busy." She smiles, though it doesn't reach her eyes. "Anyway, given that Mr. Ex lives far away now and I can't be angry with him, we'll have to find another way to get you over it."

I smirk. As I said, the breakup was pretty amicable, but Ivy seems excited, so I decide to humor her. "Like what?"

"The stuff you see in movies or books. Like... having a night out with your girlfriends."

"I'm more the type who sits at home with a book and a mug of hot cocoa."

Ivy nods. "You could burn stuff?"

"Sorry, what?" I blink, sure that my new coworker didn't just suggest arson.

"You know, burn stuff that reminds you of him. A boyfriend bonfire kinda thing."

Ivy has this wild, eager look in her eyes that makes me laugh. "I'm not sure that setting fires is the answer here."

"Well, the last option is my favorite anyway."

"What's the last option?"

Ivy leans in, drops her voice. "An adventure!"

I let out a laugh. "Now? I'm only just starting this job."

Ivy waves a hand. "If it's for love or to heal a broken heart, an adventure is mandated. And if it involves travel, all the better. Think of the places you could go. Maybe even... England!" Ivy practically swoons.

I can't help but smile. As eager as she seems to be about my apparent soon-to-be departure, I'm not sure any sort of adventure is on the cards for me at the moment.

Luckily, Ivy seems ready to drop the subject and we get into training. She gives me a rundown of the operations at the Inn and the role I'll be filling at reception. As expected, we get along well, and I find myself falling into the role easily. Another flare of excitement fills my stomach for this next step in my life.

Because New Val doesn't look back, doesn't hold onto the past. She strides forward proudly, one foot in front of the other.

6
___

ETHAN

"Sorry. Can you say that again?" I ask.

My ears are ringing, my mouth dry. I must've misheard. Because whatever Ray said just now... it can't be right.

Raymond Hall, Pops's friend and the executor of his will, peers at me over the tops of his absurdly tiny spectacles. "Which part?" he asks patiently.

"Uh... The last part."

"With the road trip treasure hunt?"

Hm. So I did hear right.

Ray theatrically removes his glasses. "It's exactly what it sounds like. Don't tell me you're surprised; this is Alfie Holmes we're talking about."

He makes a good point. I *shouldn't* be surprised. Of all the people who would incorporate a treasure hunt into their will, my granddad pretty much tops the list.

I flounder for a moment, looking out the window towards Ray's sun-soaked garden. I've never been to a will reading, and I dreaded coming to this one. It feels like an acknowledgement that Pops is really gone. And yet, him requesting that I do a final road trip adventure feels as Alfie Holmes as can be.

I stand and pace around Ray's kitchen, needing to release some anxious energy.

It feels weird to be doing this here. Movies and shows always have will readings happening in an industrial-trendy big city building with a respectably anonymous lawyer.

Instead, I'm at Ray's... who was present during my gawky teen years when my voice was mid-crack for months and I had that horrendous, swoopy Justin Bieber haircut. And whose house layout is forever imprinted on my brain from the amount of times I visited with my grandparents.

But such is life in Mirror Valley—the kind of small town where it makes sense that my granddad's best friend and will executor is also the one and only carpenter for miles around.

I clear my throat, still trying to get my bearings. "So, this road trip... what does it entail?"

Ray puts on his spectacles again and gazes down at Pops's will. "It's not a lot, would probably take a weekend. He's got a series of stops listed, and tasks to do at every location. Seems that he wants you to do one final mission without him."

I nod again, even as the backs of my eyes start to ache. "I didn't think—"

"YOOHOO!"

The screech from the front door makes me jump, but Ray barely flinches. He continues to assess the contract through his spectacles as he hollers, "In the kitchen, Franny!"

I barely have time to turn to greet the newcomer when a bundle of colorful dresses covered with an oversized jean jacket throws itself on me.

"Is that wee Ethan?!"

I give her a hug as she cackles loudly. "Hey, Fran. Good to see you."

"You too, dear boy." She steps back, but reaches up to pinch my cheek. "My goodness, there's no sense in calling you 'wee' after all. When did you get so tall? They must be feeding you well at that cooking school in Montana." Fran puts both hands to her chest, eyes wide behind her comically huge glasses.

She and Ray must have coordinated their visual accessories.

"They sure did. Though I graduated a couple months back."

"So you're a *professional chef?*" she whispers with such reverence that I have to smile. "Oo-ee how exciting! I wish Mirror Valley had a real-life fine dining restaurant with a fancy, trained chef."

Fran pinches my cheek again. She is the one and only person I allow to do that, and it's more habit than anything else. Fran was another staple of my childhood given that she worked at the fire station with my grandparents. Back then, Nana and Pops used to try and set up Fran and Ray. But to this day, no matter how close the two seniors seem to be, they both insist they're "just friends."

Val and I probably should've taken a page from their book.

"Tell me your plans," Fran chortles. "Where are you off to next? Paris? London? The Dominican? Ah, they'd all be lucky to have you!"

At this, my smile falters. I'm currently waiting to hear about the opportunity of a lifetime back in Aston Falls—a sous-chef position on the acclaimed Aston Falls Express, which is, quite literally, a restaurant on a passenger train.

Getting the job would mean that all of my efforts in

culinary school have paid off. My career would be set. It's what I've worked towards for *years*.

"Franny, please," Ray tuts. "You're embarrassing him with all your doting."

"Oh, don't be silly. He oughta be proud. I know his grandparents were." Fran's eyes go a bit misty. "Dear Alfred was so excited for you. Used to beam whenever your name came up."

I press my lips together, the light mood turning more somber. A moment of silence falls over the table as we all remember Pops.

Fran turns to Ray. "So? You told him?"

"I did."

"And is he going to do it?"

I roll my eyes, inserting myself into their discussion. "I haven't decided yet."

"But you must!" Fran takes my hand. My palm eclipses both of hers, and yet, it's very clear who has the control in this conversation. "Your granddad would want you to. Ray, did you tell him the best part?"

I hold back a smirk. I assume that will readings are normally private affairs, but of course Ray would tell Fran about this. Not that I mind, and I don't think Pops would either. Secrets in Mirror Valley always have a timer on them.

Ray's lips twitch. "Not yet."

"What's the best part?" I ask.

"Pops made one very specific request for this trip."

My mouth pinches. "Does it involve another bunny costume? No. Not after traumatizing all those kids when I came out of the lake after going to find that rogue egg. I still get messages every once in awhile from that one kid's mom—"

"No, not that." Ray files the papers together, taps them on the table. "It's something else..."

Ray stays silent. While I watch him, Fran is watching me.

The man clearly hasn't lost his flair for the dramatic.

"He wants you to do this treasure hunt with a close friend of yours. A certain person with whom you grew up..." He whips off his spectacles. "Valentina."

I sit back in my seat. "You can't be serious."

Ray turns the papers towards me, and in the same black and white, formal writing, the will reads: "This final request must be completed with Valentina Brinn Reyes-Murphy."

Like there could be another Valentina.

My brow furrows. "But why Val? Pops knew that we haven't spoken in years."

The only exception being this morning, but I'm not going to mention that.

Ray holds up his hands. "Don't look at me. This was all Alfie."

"He must've written this years ago. Before everything... happened."

"Nope. It's dated only a couple months back."

I screw up my face. *Why, Pops?*

I continue to stare at the will, as if looking at it will uncover some hidden code. "Valentina" could be an anagram for "just kidding," right?

I may not have been great at English, but even I know that's not likely.

"You should do it," Fran coaxes, taking my hand again. "Your granddad would've loved it."

Oh, sure he would. Pops was a sucker for drama.

I can't imagine Val's reaction if I approached her with this: *"Hey, Teeny. Any chance you want to be stuck in a car together for a long weekend doing a road trip to all of our favorite places before I went and broke both our hearts?"*

Yeah, no.

I'm not worried for myself, but do I really want to disrupt Val's life like that? Especially if she's happy?

And it *would* be a disruption, if this morning's interaction is anything to go by.

After everything that's happened between us, it makes sense that we don't know how to react to each other. I figured I'd see her again on this visit, I just didn't expect it to be so soon. Or for it to be so jarring. Not so much because she literally bodychecked me, but because I didn't expect how strange it would feel to see *her*.

Adult Val in all her wild-eyed, curly-haired, tiny-nosed glory.

Her nose is part of the reason I call her "Teeny." Not that I'd ever tell her that. She used to insist that she wanted an "elegant Meryl Streep nose"... whatever that means.

I wish I could say that I don't remember these things so clearly, but of course I do. Being in Aston Falls didn't exactly make me forget her, but it might've dampened the pain of not being with her.

A couple months after I left, I heard that she was in a new relationship and, last I heard, she's still with the guy. I hope he makes her happy.

My plan on this visit was, as always, to stay away from her. Give her space.

But this... could be a problem.

"And there's no alternative?" I ask. Hopefully.

Ray shrugs. "It's up to you, but the will's pretty clear on this point. Alfie left you a few things and he requested you do this treasure hunt before you receive them, but we both know he wouldn't hold you to it if you didn't want to do it."

31

"I'll do the hunt, but I'm not sure Val will. I'll have to think about asking her."

"You do that," Fran sings. She's gotten up from the table and is bustling around the kitchen, opening and closing cupboards and throwing items on the counter. "In the meantime, how about some pancakes?"

7

VAL

I'm organizing the room keys when the lobby door opens with the first check-in of the day. Ivy steps away to attend to the guest.

"Good afternoon, and welcome to the Brookrose," she says cheerily. "How may I help you?"

"I'm actually looking for someone."

The deep, pepper-grinder voice shoots through me like I spent a half-hour rubbing sock feet on carpet and then touched an electric outlet. I whirl around so fast, the keys I'm holding go flying and clatter noisily against the wall.

"You?" I burst out, my voice croaky.

Ethan is standing at the front desk. His brown eyes land on me and he smirks. "No, *you.*"

I roll my eyes. "Hilarious."

"I've got a Netflix comedy special with my name on it."

I glare at him and he just smirks back, his eyes sparking mischievously. Growing up, Ethan was a serious and responsible kid, and that private, rare sparkle used to make my heart do flips. Not anymore.

Ivy looks back and forth between us. "You two know each other?"

"Kinda." I shrug. "This is Ethan Holmes. I know him from... childhood."

Okay, I know him from a few other things (AKA we used to make out a lot) but there's no need to go into all that right after spilling my guts about Randal. Can't have Ivy thinking I'm a complete boy-crazy wreck on my first day. Especially because my mission these days is clear—Valentina Reyes-Murphy is living her best single-lady life.

Beyoncé herself has basically blessed this.

"What are you doing here?" I ask Ethan.

He opens his mouth, looks like he's going to say something, but then his gaze drops down my body. His brow puckers in a frown. "Weren't you wearing pants earlier?"

"Yeah." I don't offer further explanation.

Ethan opens his mouth and I can see the question forming on his lips—*"Why...?"* But at the last moment, he changes his mind. "I need to talk to you."

Ivy tactfully excuses herself and goes to the back office. I give her an apologetic shrug and she waves it off with a smile. Meanwhile, Ethan runs his fingers through his hair where it's hanging low over his eyes, rubs the scruff along his jawline.

I hate how handsome he is. It's really not fair. There should be rules about how attractive you can be when you see an ex.

"Look, this is kinda awkward..." Ethan starts, rubbing his jaw again.

"I'll say," I mutter under my breath.

Not quietly enough, though, because he smirks. "I *meant* that what I have to say is awkward. But actually, I won't disagree with you."

I snort, and the tension in my shoulders releases a touch. I've read about this phenomenon in my slightly cheesy (okay, *really* cheesy) "true-self discovery" books:

naming an uncomfortable emotion takes away some of its power. Apparently, it works around exes too.

Maybe I should write a book about that: "How to de-awkward the awkward: a friends-to-exes-to-friends journey."

Is this really what's important right now, Val?

"What's on your mind?" I ask, sounding appropriately breezy.

Ethan shifts. "I just came from Ray's. We went through Pops's will."

All at once, an ache shoots through me. Grief for what I've lost in Alfie's passing, but also—more so—for Ethan. I know how much he loved his grandfather.

"I'm sorry, Ethan," I say sincerely. "Pops was a good man."

"He was." He nods mechanically, looking off to the side.

I'm bothered by the faraway look in his eyes, the telltale downward quirk of his mouth. Suddenly, a gut reaction kicks in; some old habit from years ago. A distinct, primal urge to make him feel better.

Uh oh, I can't stop it. The words are coming up...

"I ripped my pants," I blurt.

That gets his attention. Ethan gives me a look. "What?"

"That's why I'm wearing Ivy's skirt." I blabber on. "I ripped my pants in the treehouse."

Ethan snorts. Laughs. My goodness, he's gorgeous when he laughs.

No, Val, he isn't. He's just a regular, normal, man-type person.

"You're hilarious, Teeny." He shakes his head. "I always loved that about you."

His compliment washes over my skin and I feel a traitorous bloom of validation that I immediately shove away.

Ethan's expression grows serious and he looks at me

curiously. The kind of look that makes goosebumps rise on my skin. "Okay, I'm going to say this fast. You don't have to say yes, definitely don't feel obligated. It's more of a formality than anything..."

Now, Ethan's the one blabbering. My palms start to sweat.

"Here goes," he mutters. Takes a deep breath. "Pops's will included his final request. He, uh, wants me to go on a road trip."

My eyebrows shoot up even as relief fills me. I thought he might bring up... Ah, it doesn't matter. "A road trip?" I say. "That's fun?"

"It is." Ethan bobs his head. "But there's a caveat. He doesn't want me to do it alone. He wants me to do it with... you."

My jaw drops. *He wants* what, *now?*

"The road trip," Ethan says quickly, his cheeks reddening as he misinterprets my shock. "He wants you to come with me."

"On a road trip. Just you and me."

"Yup. He specifically mentioned you."

A loud silence stretches between us, and I finally kick myself into gear enough to wrench my mouth shut. "Uh..." I manage intelligently.

On the one hand, of course I want to honor Alfie's legacy and do this final thing for him. He was such a feisty, clever old man with the sweetest heart you could ever imagine. It feels wrong not to do this one task he requested of me in his will.

But to do *this*, go on a trip with Ethan? Well, that has the potential of opening a whole can of sardines I'm not sure I want to be anywhere near in the first place.

"When are you..." I say, my voice creaky. "Like, when is this...?"

"I'm thinking of going this upcoming weekend," Ethan answers my half-question.

I frown. "I can't go then, I'm working. It's my first weekend on the job so I—"

"She'd *love* to!"

The tinkling voice is behind me, and is closely followed by an arm circling my shoulders. I look at Ivy, bewildered. "What?"

"She'd love to go on your road trip thing," Ivy says again, a little too cheerfully for my tastes. "We were just talking about how Val needs an adventure."

I start to shake my head. "Ivy, I couldn't. I can't leave you hanging."

"Don't be silly."

Ethan leans back. "I'll leave you two to discuss it. No pressure either way." His eyes meet mine. "But I would like it if you came, Val. For old time's sake."

With that, he walks towards the seating area and out of earshot, whistling away. Like Pops used to do.

I turn towards Ivy. "You want me to take off on a road trip when I'm supposed to be working?!"

"It's no big deal." She shrugs. "You're working the next few days, so take Friday and the weekend off. It'll be a chance for you to regroup, get yourself in order. After all, the first days of work can be *exhausting*. Consider this as part of your training."

"What would your grandparents think?"

"Ah, they won't mind another weekend if it means reuniting old friends on an adventure. They're suckers for stuff like that."

She winks at what I'm sure is a *very* skeptical expression on my part.

"Come on, it'll be good for you!" She leans towards me. "Besides, the guy *barely* looks like a serial killer. It'll be fun.

And if it's not, I'll cover any shifts you need covered for the next year."

I bite my lip. If she sees me working here for the next year even when I'm considering taking my first weekend off, I must be doing something right. "Are you absolutely sure?"

"The surest I've ever been. So, what do you say?"

∘ ∘

I said yes.

And that is why I'm standing in front of my parents' house at 6am on Friday with my bags packed, a new regency romance novel in my purse, and my stomach swirling with nerves. Ethan is in the process of backing Pops's old blue truck into the driveway.

"It's no big deal. Seriously, no big deal," I mutter, shifting back and forth on my feet.

"What was that?" Ethan calls through the driver's side window. Which, it turns out, is down so he can hear me talking to myself. Maybe he should be worried about going on this trip with *me*.

I clear my throat, try to save face. "I said those are some nice... wheels!"

I think we both know I know nothing about cars.

His rich brown eyes meet mine in the side mirror and he smirks again.

Ugh. Enough with the adorably charming smirks already!

He parks the truck, hops out, and practically frolics over to get my bags. He smiles as he approaches. "Don't you look bright-eyed and bushy-tailed this morning."

"And *you* can pack up that cheery attitude of yours and take it elsewhere," I grumble, then immediately feel bad as he places my bags into the trunk. "Sorry, that was rude. Still not a morning person."

"I figured," Ethan says, undeterred. He goes to the front of the truck and proffers a metal thermos. "Coffee?"

My hand shoots out like I've found my oasis in the desert. "Thank you, thank you. I didn't want to wake my parents by making coffee at this hour."

"Thought you might need it. And I also brought..."

He reaches back into the truck, grabs a Tupperware, and opens it. A rich, sugary sweet, chocolatey scent fills my nostrils and I moan despite myself. "Is that...?"

"Brownies? Absolutely."

He takes a napkin, picks up a brownie with far more restraint than I'd have, and holds it out to me. I take it eagerly, try not to notice the way Ethan licks the sticky chocolate off his fingers with that perfect mouth of his.

I can't believe I used to kiss that mouth.

Not that that's *at all* relevant to what we're doing.

I've been trying to look at the bright side of this hapless adventure. Ethan and I texted through the week to organize ourselves—because of course he still has my childhood number memorized despite the fact that we haven't texted in years—and I've come around to thinking that this trip is an opportunity for us to reestablish our friendship and move past the awkward limbo stage.

I'm tired of the lengths I've had to go to in order to avoid him over the years. If I no longer have to dive behind snow-drifts, or bushes, or groups of children, my life would be better for it.

Besides, New Val wouldn't dare pull a muscle hiding from an ex. So patching things up with Ethan and putting the past in the past is another way to move forward.

We've already taken the first step by acknowledging the awkwardness. Now, it's a question of becoming some-what friendly again. Not to say that I think we'll ever be as close as we once were. Or that I would want to be.

After what happened, I fully intend to keep him at arm's length.

Just need to get my wayward mouth thoughts under control.

"So what's our first stop?" I ask in a very friend-ish way as Ethan circles the car and opens the door for me.

"If I tell you, I'll have to kill you."

I sigh tiredly. "I've never met anyone below the age of forty-seven who makes so many corny dad jokes."

Ethan gives me another smirk. "Classic Pops. He's structured this as a bit of a treasure hunt."

I shift, my heart suddenly racing. "A treasure hunt?"

"Yeah." Ethan pauses, shoots a glance my way. "That okay?"

I almost say no. Almost dive out of the car. But my hands feel tied. This is Pops' final request... no matter how uncomfortable I feel about it at the moment. I tug on my seatbelt with a touch more force than necessary. "Yeah, sure. Of course."

"Great. We're going to play paintball."

My hands freeze around the seatbelt. "*Paintball?* As in... shooting at each other with dangerous rainbow pellet guns?!"

"That's the one."

"And do we actually have to... participate?"

"Yup."

My mouth turns down. I've never played paintball, was conveniently sick or busy or unavailable whenever Ethan and his friends had plans to play. Why Pops wanted me along for this particular portion of the trip, I have no idea.

Ethan shoots me a glance as he starts the car. "What? Scared I'm gonna beat you?"

"Not in a million years," I say, all bravado. I turn to grab the Tupperware from the backseat. "But if I'm going to be kicking your butt soon, I need to restore my energy."

I open the container and practically faint once again at the chocolatey goodness. I reach in and take a big slice, licking my lips.

"Glad to see you're still into brownies." Ethan chuckles.

"I've actually diversified my brownie portfolio over the years. Raspberry, red velvet, blondies... The ones I can't get on board with are peanut butter brownies." I shudder at the memory of the ones I tried a few weeks back. They were dry, heavy on the salt. Disappointing.

"I'll have to try my hand at those ones when I get some time to bake."

"Don't do it as much anymore, huh? Too busy living the high life in Aston Falls?" Hmm. That was meant to be light-hearted, but it came out a *touch* bitter and resentful. Maybe I'm not quite as over everything as I thought I was. "Sorry, I didn't mean for that to sound harsh."

"You're fine, Teeny. And you're right. Life's been a lot lately, but I do miss baking. It was, like, my relaxation time. Well, that and the gym."

He flexes his tanned, muscular biceps in a joking manner. I roll my eyes. "I'll never understand it."

"Understand what?"

"You're a chef. You eat delicious food all the time, and you clearly love baking."

"Correct on all counts."

"So how on earth do you manage to keep in shape? If I was eating nonstop brownies and cheese and butter, I would *not* look like that."

Ethan waggles his eyebrows. "Look like what, Teeny?"

Oh, no! I definitely didn't want to sound flirty. Back-track, backtrack!

"No!" I sputter. "I mean... I didn't think..."

"I'm giving you a hard time." Ethan smirks. "Way I see it, you should eat the things you love and do what makes you feel good. Life's tough, why deprive yourself of the things that bring you joy?"

I lick the final crumbs off my lips. "You're wise for your age."

Ethan's gaze drops to my mouth briefly, and when he speaks again, his voice is pensive. "Loss is a good teacher."

There's a slight tightening at the corner of his eyes, and his lips press into a line. This close, I see the freckles across his cheekbone, the way his scruff is growing in almost auburn near his chin.

There really is something different about him. He's more world-wary, has this sort of cautious alertness to him. Maybe he's just more mature.

He shoots me a glance, and I abruptly look away. "You were a good teacher too, that one time."

"Which time?" I ask innocently. "There are *so many* to choose from."

"You know the one. That day in front of my house."

I give my head a shake. "I still can't believe *I* was the one to teach you that."

"It took a few tries, but look at me now." Ethan taps the stick, shifts from second to third gear.

I sigh loudly, even as my chest feels heavy.

Of course I remember that day. It was the same day everything changed.

8

VAL

Four Years Ago

The church services went pretty much as expected.

Carmen and Alicia spent the first fifteen minutes squabbling over who got to wear the precious pink hair bow today (there's only one, and clearly, it's in high demand), while my oldest brother Pete tried unsuccessfully to budge me over so he wouldn't have to sit next to Mrs. Nonstop-Chatter (Mrs. Finlay is an absolute dear, but she will talk your ear off for a good two hours if you let her).

Meanwhile, I sat quietly in the pew, trying and failing to read my book. I probably should've been reading *The Book* while waiting for Pastor Holden to start his sermon, but I'm at *such* a good part.

As much as I love my family, they're a little nuts. It's part of the reason I love the treehouse and Ethan's grand-parents' place. There's so much silence, so much order. Nothing like my house, which is practically the family-home equivalent of an elephant in a china shop. Or however the expression goes.

Which is why, two and a half hours later, I'm escaping

my house again. Carmen and Alicia never settled their bow fight and the conflict has escalated to include the time Alicia "accidentally on purpose" read Carmen's diary. This time, Mom's playing mediator while Dad clangs around the garage fixing the car so my other brother Simon can drive it to his softball tournament.

All I want to do is finish my chapter.

Now clad in my favorite shorts and a white T-shirt, I set off towards Ethan's grandparents' house on the outskirts of town. As I turn onto the deserted stretch of road—recently paved for a new housing development—I spot Ethan's bike on the front lawn. With his mom working nights, she usually stays up in the mornings to see Ethan, then sleeps through the afternoons. Which means that Ethan's here for the rest of the day, either baking something delicious with his grandma, or helping Pops with odd jobs and/or treasure hunts.

And there are a *lot* of treasure hunts. Since retiring from the fire department, Pops has full rein to answer to his life's calling.

I approach the house and am surprised to see that the garage door's open. In all my years coming here, I think I've seen it open a total of eight times. Alfie's prized blue pickup always gets the prestigious, temperature-controlled garage spot, while his beat-up station wagon sits in the driveway to freeze through the winters.

"Hello?" I call, but I don't see anyone. In fact, it's almost suspiciously quiet.

Then, I notice that the pickup is moving. Backing down the driveway.

Pops must be going somewhere. I step out of the way and raise a hand to wave.

As it rolls past me, my jaw pops open.

The driver's seat is empty.

"NOO!"

I swivel to see Ethan sprinting down the driveway, a string of expletives coming from his mouth.

"Stop the truck!" he bellows as he runs into the empty street.

My reflexes kick into gear and I follow him at a run. Not that it's necessary... the truck's going maybe two miles an hour.

He braces himself against the back bumper, and I join him. The truck comes to a stop.

"What happened?" I gasp, shoving my hip into the bumper.

"Emergency brake," Ethan grunts, frowning as he rubs his jaw. He's shaved since this morning. "Why did I release the emergency brake?"

"Yeah, that was stupid."

"It was in first gear, though." He's staring at the pickup like it personally offended him. "It wasn't meant to roll."

I unstick myself from the bumper and go around the side. "It's in neutral."

Ethan's eyes widen and he looks so perplexed for a moment, I almost burst into laughter. He lets out another few curse words as he comes around to the passenger side and firmly raises the emergency brake.

"What are you doing with the truck anyway?" I ask. Ethan's hilariously awful at driving manual transmission. Or it would be hilarious, if it wasn't alarming that he was clearly planning on taking the truck out alone.

"I was going to teach myself to drive it. Pops gave me enough pointers, I think I can do it." He bites the inside of his cheek. "It was for tonight. Meant to be part of your surprise."

I blink innocently. "To crash Pops's precious baby? Oh, shucks. You shouldn't have."

He gives me a look.

I smile sweetly, then gesture at the pickup. "Get in. I'll teach you."

"*You* want to teach *me* how to drive stick shift?"

"No. *I* want to teach *you* not to run over pedestrians."

Ethan rolls his eyes. "It's just that..." He looks at the ground and shifts. "You know..."

"What?"

"You're the worst backseat driver."

"Excuse me?"

"You start off all nice and sweet, but then..." He gestures with his hands. "There's a lot of shouting in other languages. Not only Spanish. I've heard French, Romanian... I swear you spoke Arabic once."

My cheeks heat and I purse my lips. "It was one time. A few words I learned from Tara in school. I can't even remember them anymore."

He snorts. "Yeah, well... can you blame me for being hesitant?"

"Come on, don't be a baby," I taunt him. "I'll teach you."

"Alright. But if this leads to tears, I want it known that I was hesitant."

"Don't worry, I won't cry."

"I wasn't talking about you." He cocks an eyebrow.

I circle around to the passenger side while he climbs into the driver's seat. It's a big truck; my feet almost dangle off the floor. I give Ethan a short rundown of what to do, how to slowly release the clutch while pressing the gas.

He stares at the gear shift. "So I have to press the clutch, release, then move the gear shift?"

There's a little crinkle between his eyes that I half want to kiss, half want to rub away. "Not quite. You have to press the clutch, move the gear shift, then slowly, *slowly* release."

Ethan blows out a breath. "I think I need to try it."

He starts the pickup, gets it into first gear...

Stalls immediately.

"What'd I do?" he asks, running his hands through his hair.

"You released the clutch too fast. Try it again."

Ethan restarts the engine, moves the stick shift into first gear, releases the clutch and...

Stalls.

"Argh," he grumbles, uttering a few more choice words.

I sigh, shaking my head. Ethan is your trademark "learn by doing" kind of person; it's one of the qualities that'll make him ace culinary school. His muscle memory is something else, and once he knows how to do something, it's incredible how perfectly he can duplicate that action.

"Okay..." I say. "I have an idea."

"What?"

"Don't make a big deal out of it." My cheeks are warm as I undo my seatbelt and come around the truck. Open the driver's door. "I'm going to show you how to do it. Just mirror my movements."

I kick off my flip-flops, climb into the seat with him, and sit squarely on his lap. He doesn't seem particularly surprised or affected by how close we are right now; he only adjusts me so I'm comfortable on his thighs.

I try my best not to notice the way his warm, cozy smell makes me want to curl up against his chest and take a nap. I clear my throat and straighten up, a little lightheaded by the feeling of his body against mine.

Ethan places his arms around me loosely, all business.

"So what do I do?" he asks. His breath on the back of my neck sends shivers across my skin.

I remind myself to stay focused. My spine is ramrod

straight as I firmly grasp his hands and put one on the steering wheel, the other on the key. "Let's start the car."

I press my feet into his so he's pushing down on both the clutch and the brake. Then, we start the engine.

"Good," I say. "Now, let's shift into first gear."

I place his hand on the stick shift, move the car into first gear.

"Give the car a little gas, and slowly release the clutch."

I'm invested now, wanting Ethan to get this right. I move my foot towards the gas and he mirrors the movement. Then, with my left foot, we very slowly release the clutch. I feel his foot press up against mine but I hold firm.

Soon, we're rolling forward… somewhat smoothly.

"You're doing it!" I squeal.

"Ha!" He sounds so excited, my heart glows.

We pick up speed along the deserted road heading nowhere, and Ethan turns the truck around. I sit slightly to one side so I'm not obstructing his view.

"Ready to go into second gear?" he asks.

"Absolutely." I take his hand on the gear shift again and put my feet back on top of his. We press the clutch, move the stick into second gear, and then slowly release.

The truck speeds up with a small jolt.

Ethan turns the truck again, and we pick up speed. Soon enough, the engine is revving loudly and he wants to move into third gear. This time, I keep my hands and feet to myself, and balance on his lap. He moves into third gear seamlessly.

"You've got it!" I exclaim.

We reach the driveway to his grandparents' house again and he rolls the truck to a stop.

"Val!" He wraps his arms around my waist and pulls me against him. "Thank you! No matter how many times Pops tried to show me, I couldn't get it."

I giggle as he showers my face and neck with kisses. "Happy to help."

"Besides." He nuzzles my ear, sending shockwaves down my spine. "I'd much rather have *you* on my lap."

I laugh, a little breathless, and his lips meet mine again. His hands tangle in my hair and he brings me close, deepening the kiss. Any inkling of laughter disappears as I lean into him, spreading my hands across his chest so I can feel his strong heartbeat beneath my palms...

Knock knock!

Ethan and I both startle. Turn towards the window.

Alfie is staring at us with an eyebrow raised. He's trying to be serious, but his lips twitch with amusement. "What do you two think you're doing?"

9

ETHAN

What in the world do I think I'm doing?

Val is sitting next to me in the truck, munching away on another brownie, and all I can think about is how close she is to me right now. How her arm almost grazes mine when she brushes back her hair. How the smell of her pomegranate shampoo is making me feel things I have no business feeling.

And the way she's licking those full lips of hers. Lips I'll never forget having against mine...

"So!" I burst out so suddenly that Val jumps in her seat. Yes, if I'm talking, I can't think about her lips. "How's life? Catch me up."

Val snorts. "Catch you up? What are you, a gossipy Real Housewife?"

"What gave it away?" I deadpan.

"Your nails and perfect hair flip."

I imitate flipping my hair over my shoulder.

"Hmm, too much flair. It's more like this."

Too late, I realize this was a mistake. Val dramatically throws her hair back and pomegranate washes over me. My heart slams and I force myself to keep my eyes on the road and not look at what I'm sure is her teasing smile.

"Nailed it." I say, my voice thick. I take a sip of coffee, clear my throat.

What're you doing, Ethan? You can't have thoughts like this anymore.

These are just habits. Remnants from the days we were dating. Like muscle memory.

Nothing more, nothing less.

"How's the family?" I ask, sounding more normal.

"Good." I hear the smile in her voice as she settles back in her seat. She rolls down her window and her hand makes waves in the wind. A wind which, thankfully, is dissipating her fruity, sexy scent. "Alicia's still in LA, and Simon's moved to Chicago for law school. Oh! Carmen got accepted to college in Summer Lakes, so she's moving soon."

"And your mom and dad?"

"Same old. Dad's *obsessed* with his model trains; it's so endearing. And Mom's started selling her carrots at the market every Thursday night."

"No more raccoon fights then?"

I immediately regret my words. Val probably doesn't even remember that conversation.

But she snorts. "No more raccoon fights."

A loaded silence settles between us. A silence that makes me want to glance at her, but I resist. There's a lot unsaid between Val and me, and I want to bridge the gap. I wish there was a way to tell her how much I regret leaving the way I did. Instead, I settle for asking, "Any other note-worthy news?"

"I was dating someone," she blurts. "Randal. Remember him? From math class?"

I nod stiffly, my throat suddenly tight. Of course I

remember him; he's been her boyfriend for the past four years. As much as I knew I shouldn't, I kept track of her. I heard through the grapevine that she began dating Randal Hamlin in senior year, only a couple months after we broke up.

I felt it justified my actions. Proved that we weren't meant to be. Proved that Val was better off without me. And as long as she was happy, I could find a way to be happy. Even if the thought of her with someone else broke me.

"I remember him," I say with a nod. "I mean, I didn't actually know the guy, but as long as you're happy and he treats you right—"

"*Treated* me right," Val tacks on quietly. "He did, mostly. We... broke up earlier this year."

My heart leaps. I fiercely and firmly make it stop. "Sorry to hear that."

"Don't be. It was for the best, and a long time coming." She frowns, and her hand stops making waves. "We were together for so long, but I never really felt like I knew him. You know?"

I relax into the seat. I know I shouldn't care about this stuff, but hearing Val be open and honest like this, even about someone she used to date... well, it softens me a little. Reminds me of the days when we used to share everything with each other.

"Sorry." She chuckles dryly and resumes her hand waving motions. "That was TMI. I don't know why I'm talking to you about this."

"It's okay," I say, and I mean it. I like hearing Val's internal monologue after so long without it.

"Anyway. After Randal and I ended, I made a decision. I jumped into that relationship so fast... Too fast. So I've decided that I'm going to be single for awhile." She bobs her head firmly. "Totally single. Find my true self. You know?"

I grin, risk a glance her way. "Absolutely. You should do what feels right for you."

What I don't tell her is that I've been doing my very own "process of self-discovery" lately... as in, I haven't dated anyone in awhile. No one has really sparked my interest past the first or second date. If that.

I glance at Val again. See the small, dreamy smile on her face, the way her amber eyes light up as she scans the road ahead. She's kicked off her shoes and her feet are up on the dash. She's wearing these pink denim shorts that make my head spin.

I wish she didn't have this effect on me anymore.

"AGH!" Val pulls her hand back into the truck. "Something hit me!"

I look at her full on. "What?!"

"Something..." she trails off as she looks at her hand.

I follow her eyes, and then burst into abrupt laughter. "Is that—?"

"DON'T say it! Don't even think it."

"Val..." I'm laughing so hard, I might have to pull over. "That's—"

"Bird poo?" she says, nostrils flaring. "Yeah, got it. Do you have a—"

"Towel's in the back."

She undoes her seatbelt with one hand and turns in her seat. As she scrambles into the back, she leans so close that my laugher catches in my chest.

With a grimace, she sits back down and grumbles as she wipes off the white splatter. Wipes again and again so the top of her hand is red. "Ew, ew, ew!"

"They say that's a sign of good luck."

"*They* are just trying to make people who get hit with poo feel better," she responds flatly. "An impossible mission, by the way."

"There's hand sanitizer in the passenger door."

"Thanks." She pumps out a solid five dollops. Shoots me a suspicious look. "You're prepared."

A smirk crosses my lips. "I never forgot your streak of bad luck."

Though I'm looking at the road, I physically feel Val tense up next to me. "I don't have bad luck," she squeaks indignantly. "Not anymore."

"So the ripped pants, and the bird poo are...?"

"Unfortunate, unrelated incidents about which you have no business making assumptions." She shifts in her seat and looks out the window.

Hm. I clearly touched a nerve. Val used to laugh with me whenever bad things happened to either of us, but apparently that's a line I can no longer cross.

"I'm sorry," I say sincerely. "Really. I shouldn't have brought it up."

"Yes. Well. Things are different now."

She's so right, and so wrong, all at once.

10

ETHAN

"Don't touch." Pops smacks my hand away. Like I'm a toddler.

I chuckle. "It's for scientific purposes!"

"Can't let you take that kind of risk." He shakes a finger at me. Then, he takes that finger, turns around, and sticks it into the brownie batter himself. He licks off the gooey, chocolatey substance, and smacks his lips, giving me a satisfied smile. "It's safe. You can go ahead."

I roll my eyes. "Thanks for looking out."

Pops laughs. "Where's Val?"

"In my room. A friend from school called her for help with some boy problem. I tried to give advice, but Val shushed me. Said I didn't know what I was talking about."

Thing is, I know *exactly* what I'm talking about because Noah Jackson—the alleged crush—is my gym buddy. But clearly, that doesn't matter. There's a precise, highly-intelligent, strategized system of crush-hunting in girls' minds that I could never wrap my own head around.

I've sometimes wondered if that's how Val got me

wrapped around her finger. Then realized that I've been wrapped around her finger as long as I can remember.

I take a teaspoon to try a small bite of the batter. After considering it for a few moments, I add a couple more shakes of salt to bring out the flavors of the chocolate. Nana always leaves me with the batter before we stick whatever we're making in the oven. She says I should be a baked good sommelier.

Dream job, if I ever heard one.

Being a chef sounds great, but it's also the practical choice. Working in fine dining restaurants brings in a good buck, which means that I'll be able to help support my family and take some of the stress off my mom. She's put on a brave face over the years, and I wanted for nothing, but I saw the toll it was taking on her. Noticed the late nights she spent going through bills and pinching pennies where she could. Being able to take some of the burden off her shoulders is important to me.

"You two..." Pops chuckles, shaking his head. "You remind me of Nana and me."

His eyes dance and my neck gets hot as I remember him knocking on the car window earlier. Anytime I so much as think about having Val on my lap when we were driving, it's all I can do not to want to take her in my arms again. Or take a cold shower.

I'm so drawn to her sometimes. I can hardly believe my luck that we're together.

"She's alright," I say, playing it cool.

Pops makes a "psh" sound, not falling for it. "She's wonderful, son. One of a kind. Why she puts up with the likes of you, I'll never know."

He elbows me teasingly and I laugh with him. Then my stomach squeezes with nerves. "Thanks for your help getting things ready for tonight."

"My pleasure. And you should thank Ray, too. It'll be quite the surprise." Pops smacks my shoulder good-naturedly, but I see the emotion in his blue eyes. "You and Val are wonderful together."

"I think so." I smile. "I hope she feels the same."

"I'm sure she does. Life has its ups and downs, but with the right partner, you'll make it through. That's why it's so wonderful that you and Val are such good friends. You have that solid base to fall back on, and you don't want to lose that, son. Chemistry, passion, all that will come and go. But a rock-solid friendship will carry you through the hard times."

"So you think I'm doing the right thing? With this pre-posal, I mean?"

Pops smiles. "I think that life's too short not to take a chance on the things that make you happy."

11

VAL

I am NOT happy about this.

When I get up there, I'm coming for you, Alfie.

I'm in the change room at the paintball field, grunting and struggling into the horrendous navy overall things we're required to wear. Mine are too small in the butt and shoulder regions, but apparently, beggars can't be choosers when it comes to stiff and over-starched paint-covered jumpsuits.

Seems they don't get many girls here as this is a "Boys Youth XL" size.

I'm choosing not to read into that.

Ethan's in the change room next to mine, but from the lack of sound, his coveralls fit just fine. Or maybe he's out already and chatting with the heavily-bearded guy behind the counter. Beardy seemed mildly surprised that we arrived in time for our "appointment."

Yeah, he called it that. As if this was a doctor's office and not a big, industrial warehouse that smells like feet and tears.

I know, I'm being grouchy. But if I'm honest, what Ethan said in the car is still bothering me.

I'm trying so hard to be put together these days. To be the "New Val"—the adult who wears nice suits, and is bravely herself, and is that enviable Girlboss level of cool, calm and confident. Ethan mentioning my "streak of bad luck" made me feel like I was back at square one.

But I will lift my head high and "fake it 'til I make it," per Rih Rih's wise advice on TikTok. Because this is a one-time paintball situation, and if that isn't the case (unlikely), New Val will certainly purchase her own cute and clean paintball outfit before setting foot in a place like this again.

With that thought in mind, I stick my arm through the left sleeve of my stupid "Boys XL" coveralls, determined to play it as cool as I can given the circumstances.

At that moment, I notice something in the corner. Something that I *thought* was just a patch of algae (don't ask why I thought algae would be found in the midst of the Colorado mountains).

Unfortunately, I can now confirm that it isn't algae.

Because it's moving. And it's coming right at me.

My breath catches in my chest for two horrific, world-ending, slow-motion seconds. Then...

"EEEEEEE!"

I barrel out of the change room. Trip on the curtain and fly forward, right coverall sleeve flapping in the wind as I tumble towards the ground.

Then, Ethan's right in front of me. Catching me again.

"It's over there! There's a... it's huge!" I'm panting, eyes wide as I stare in horror at the change room. I take a moment to thank my lucky stars that I'm still wearing my white tank top. Though the "Boys XL" tag is probably on display for everyone and anyone to see.

"What?" Ethan asks, his grip firm as he keeps me from basically crawling on top of him.

"A spi–spider!" I sputter. "In the change room!"

Ethan freezes for a breath, then relaxes in a laugh. It's at that moment that I realize his coveralls are also only half done-up, and he's wearing a gray undershirt. His bare, muscled arms are wrapped tight around me, holding me against him. On his right forearm, I see the edge of a small tattoo.

Hm. That's new.

His firewood scent surrounds me and suddenly I'm not thinking of the tattoo, or paintball, or the spider anymore. All I can feel is his chest rising and falling beneath my palms, hear his heartbeat near my cheek.

A wave of heat courses through my body. I force myself to push away, but this proves to be a bad idea as I'm now staring into those warm, dark brown eyes. Eyes swirling with something intense and smoldering...

I give my head a shake and take a HUGE step backwards. Because no, Ethan's eyes are not and will never again *smolder*.

"I'll take care of it," he says. He walks towards the change room and my traitor gaze follows his every movement.

Until I realize what he's about to do.

"Don't kill it!" I shout. "Just trap it and carry it out."

Ethan throws a glance over his shoulder, another smirk that makes my stomach do a series of flutters. "I wouldn't, Val. You know I wouldn't."

12

ETHAN

"Shoot!" I holler. "You have a clear shot!"

Val stares at her paintball gun in confusion. "How do you work this thing?!"

She continues to fiddle with the hopper on her gun. I consider going over to help her, but if I know Val, she won't want my help. Not at this stage anyway. She likes to give things a good try before she asks for outside assistance.

It's both one of her most admirable and infuriating qualities.

"Don't worry about it." I shake my head. "He got away."

Val follows my gaze to where the boy is currently skittering off behind a haybale. He high-fives his friends and they burst into raucous laughter.

How we got paired up to play against this group of kids, I'll never know. But it's Val and me against four power-hungry, loud-mouthed, prepubescent teen boys and one girl. Who keeps looking around with her nose crinkled and rolling her eyes at a boy I can only assume is her brother.

"Grrr," Val grunts again.

Then, something clicks. She smiles.

Points the gun straight at me.

My hands go up. "Hey, what're you–?"

She shoots. A splotch of pink spreads on the ground close to my feet. I look up at her and she's smiling angelically.

"Oops," she says sweetly, eyes dancing.

"You little..."

I don't finish my sentence. Before I can think about what I'm doing, I'm lunging forward and grabbing her around the waist. Val reacts immediately, squealing and wriggling out of my grasp. I chase her around, hopping over haybales and ducking behind paint-covered pieces of plaster.

For a minute, it feels like we're kids again, like no time has passed at all. Like we're just Val and Ethan; not estranged-childhood-friend-exes.

Suddenly, white paint splatters on the wall behind me. A blob of yellow narrowly misses Val's arm.

Right, we're actually in competition. With other people.

"Duck!" I take Val's hand and pull her ahead of me to protect her from any more shots. I drag her behind a haybale and we scramble to take cover, resting our backs against the itchy straw.

"That was close," Val pants. "They almost got us."

"Well, if *someone* hadn't gone rogue..."

"I was making sure you were on your game. C minus, by the way."

I chuckle, not missing her smile. And at that moment— her dark hair full of straw and her cheeks pink from running —I'm absolutely certain no one has ever looked so good in paint-covered overalls.

I have to resist a sudden urge to pull her close, like I used to. But we're not kids anymore, and we certainly aren't together.

Val peeks out from behind the haybale. "Dang it. Looks

like they've built themselves a haybale fortress. They're..." She pauses. Sighs tiredly. "Making faces and imitating us running away."

I look out. The boys are literally tripping over themselves doing this bizarre, exaggerated run while guffawing with laughter. I smirk, remembering my own teen years. I guess it's good that these kids are having fun, even if it's at our expense. Plus, it gives us an opportunity for strategizing.

Or it would... if the group wasn't covered by the makeshift shelter. "We don't have a clear shot," I mutter.

"Nope. Although, do you see the girl?"

My eyes skate over the group—four boys, but not a fifth person. "Where is she?"

There's no answer.

"Val?" I turn towards her. She doesn't move, just stares ahead at something I can't make out.

I move closer to her, on high alert. Then, I see it.

The girl's crouched behind a piece of plaster not far from us. She hasn't seen us yet, and she peeks out periodically. It looks like she wants to get back to the group of boys, but is worried we'll catch her.

Which we could do. Val has a direct shot.

At that moment, the girl's eyes land on us and her face pales. She looks young, probably no more than twelve. Her red hair is gathered in a braid and she's wearing glasses that sit slightly lopsided on her face.

Her gaze drops to Val, who appears to be mouthing something at her. The girl looks suspicious, her lips twisted down.

I don't miss what Val mouths next: "*Go on.*"

Something like hope crosses the girl's face, then she looks at me. I give her a nod.

She flashes her braces at us in a grateful smile and launches forward. She darts, cat-like, towards the boys and into their little shelter. There's a chorus of cheers and whoops as the group is reunited.

Val sits back against the straw, smiling.

"What was that about?" I ask.

"We've all felt out of our depths at some point." She shrugs. "I figured she could use a win."

Val goes back to adjusting her hopper, but my gaze lingers on her. My heart warms at her kindness. Same old Val—always looking out for everyone else. She used to be inspire me to be better, to put others before myself.

I hope that ex of hers put *her* first, made her a priority. Like I should've done.

"I fixed the ladder, by the way," I say quietly, without thinking.

"What?"

"The rope ladder to the treehouse. I bought a new one and set it up a couple days ago." I shift against the straw, unsure exactly why I'm telling Val this but wanting her to know. "Fixed the spider hole in the wall, too. And changed the bulbs in the fairy lights."

Val tilts her head. "Why'd you do that?"

My brow puckers. It's a good question, actually. I hadn't thought much about it. I just did it. "I don't know... I have lots of good memories there. I figured it was worth maintaining."

Val stares at me for a long moment, expressionless. Then, her face breaks into this full, genuine, sweet smile, and her eyes fill with a joy that makes my heart pound.

That's why, a small voice says in my head.

In the light of Val's smile, I feel a sudden, deep need to say something. Something I've wanted to tell her for ages, and something she needs to hear. My voice goes serious. "Val, about what happened that summer—"

"C'mon, lovebirds!" one of the kids cuts me off. "We're getting bored. Quit making out already!"

I tense up and Val freezes. There's a long beat where neither of us moves.

Then her lips quirk up into a mischievous little smile.

I know exactly what she's thinking.

"Ready?" I whisper, clicking the safety off my paintball gun.

Val nods slowly. "Let's do it."

"3... 2... 1!"

Val and I shoot to a stand. We dart around our protective barrier and come towards the haybale fortress in a full frontal attack.

13

VAL

"*About what happened that summer.*"

Oh, my giddy gosh. He wasn't about to...? He wouldn't have...?

Smack!!

My head bounces off the passenger window and I wince, remembering at the last minute to keep my eyes closed.

Ugh. Pretending to sleep in a car driving on a gravel road is a challenge. I'm proud of my ability to nap in most places—planes, trains, airports... even on a slow-moving roller coaster once. But as my head crashes into the window again, I'm not sure I can keep this up.

I make a little grunting noise and shift in my seat, placing my head on the headrest. *Sweet relief!*

Now, back to regularly-scheduled programming... AKA freaking out over what Ethan almost said on the paintball field.

What brought it on anyway? Was he going to say what I think he was going to say and bring up our breakup? I always assumed that conversation was dead and buried, but here he is, calling it forth from the beyond. Summoning up ghosts.

I like true crime as much as the next person, but this is all a bit too Deja Breakup for me.

Though it was for the best that he brought me back down to earth. For a minute there, it felt like old times, back when things between us were light and fun and bantery. I loved that about Ethan and me. But there was an almost flirtatious edge to the whole him-chasing-me-around-with-a-paintball-gun thing, and that aspect must be thrown away like yesterday's bread.

I'm going to take it as a win, in the grand scheme of things. Ethan and I are simply approaching something like friendship again, which should reduce any and all awkwardness in the future. I simply must remember not to flirt with him... or to interpret his teasing as flirting. It's too dangerous to go down that road again, to entertain something that could never be.

So, it's settled. Ethan and I will continue to have a good, friendly time, and I will feel zero sparks. I will be a lake, tap water, and other flat, wet things.

Flat and wet. That's me.

14

ETHAN

S *nnooRRRrrre!!!*

I glance at Val, who I can confirm is now definitely asleep. Her head is arched back against the headrest and her mouth is wide open.

We've moved from the gravel road onto the highway, and I'm grateful. Val can sleep through a tornado, but the way her head was banging against the passenger window every two minutes had me concerned. If she really *was* sleeping through that, I'd have to let sleep scientists know of this medical marvel.

SSSSSSnooRRRRe!

Aw. Just roaring away like a small, wild-haired lawnmower.

I'm glad she's sleeping. It's giving me space and time to consider what happened when we were playing paintball... which is that I came to a realization. It's not particularly momentous or ground-breaking, but it surprises me how certain I am:

I'm still into Val. Have never stopped being into her. She still flips my stomach with a single glance, still feels like the best friend and partner (paintball or otherwise) that I could ever have.

Growing up, I had to be responsible, take things so seriously. It was only Mom and me, so she was candid about what she needed from me, and I did everything I could to help her. We were a team, we worked well together. But with Val, I could be a kid. *She* was my childhood in so many ways. Our stupid inside jokes, the letter box, games only we knew how to play...

She was my escape, but it went deeper than that. With Val, I could be myself; I never had to put on a front, or act a certain way. I appreciated that about us. I wonder if we could ever get back to that point.

Was a haybale-strewn paintball field the best place to bring up our past? Probably not. So I'm thanking all the teen boy overlords for that interruption. I can't assume that Val has residual feelings for me, especially after what I did. Just because I never got over her doesn't mean it goes both ways.

But maybe Pops was onto something with this last cunning plan of his. Maybe this is my opportunity to correct my mistakes and make amends. Maybe this is my last chance to spend real, proper time with the first—and only—girl I ever loved.

A last chance road trip, of sorts.

At that moment, my phone buzzes. My heart picks up when I see who the email's from—Carolyn at the Aston Falls Express. The subject line reads: "Following up on your application..."

I still can't believe that I'm in the final round for the sous-chef position.

I'm excited. Really, I am. This is what I've wanted for so long. Granted, the reasons I want to be a chef have changed —Mom's job in Aston Falls pays really well now, and between that and the work I've done in restaurants over the years, we were able to support my grandparents through their retirement. But this job is one-of-a-kind. A great, completely unique opportunity.

snnooooOORRe!!!

I smirk as I glance at Val.

And it suddenly occurs to me that, as excited as I am about this sous-chef position, I'm even more excited to be here right now with her... Even if she is snoring so loud, the truck's practically shaking.

I'll get back to Carolyn after this weekend, I decide. For this weekend, I'm off the grid.

And speaking of going off the grid...

I spot a familiar exit up ahead. It isn't part of the road trip, but I've been meaning to stop by since I got back to town. And with all this reminiscing about my grandparents, it feels almost fated that we'd stop here.

I signal right and turn off the highway. Hopefully Val won't mind if we make a detour.

15

VAL

S *nuuuuURRRFFFFFF!*

I jerk to wakefulness, completely disoriented. The back of my neck aches and my mouth is dry. Where am I??

It takes one long second to realize that I'm in the car. Another second to realize that it's not just any car, but Ethan's granddad's precious blue pickup.

Oh, say it ain't so...

I snored myself awake. Yeah, I was that loud. Fantastic.

But the magical bug must be watching over me because it looks like Ethan's not here. In fact, the truck's stopped and he's nowhere to be seen.

Ivy will be thrilled to hear that, while Ethan isn't a serial killer, he is a kidnapper. Not that I'm a kid anymore.

He's a friendnapper. Or I'm the friend-napper.

UGH. His corny jokes are rubbing off on me.

We're parked in a lot facing a row of tall elm trees with yellow and orange leaves. In a couple weeks' time, the ground will be covered with them as the world turns a cozy golden hue. I love when the fall breeze blows out all the muggy summer air. I'd appreciate it a lot more right now if it weren't for the alarming friend-napping situation.

There are a few cars parked next to ours, and as I look around, I recognize where we are.

Yes, I see why Ethan stopped here.

I hop out of the truck and follow the stone pathway between the trees. The air is still today, or maybe it's the feel of this place. There's no wind, no movement in the leaves except the occasional bird flitting from branch to branch. The smells of late summer fill my nostrils as I make my way through the park.

He's exactly where I knew he'd be—standing at the edge of the grass closest to the pond. In front of his grandma's gravestone.

I walk up next to him without a word. He doesn't turn to me, just says, "I didn't want to wake you."

"I figured," I say, ignoring the slight heat in my cheeks at the thought of my embarrassing snoring. It doesn't matter right now.

He's silent for a moment. "This isn't part of the trip, in case you were wondering. I thought it'd be nice to stop by. Hope that's alright."

"Of course, Ethan." I shoot him a look. "I'm glad you stopped."

Another silence settles between us as we stand at the gravestone. I take a moment to remember Ethan's grandma, and send a little prayer to the heavens for her. I don't go to church as much as I used to, but my faith is still important to me. Despite my magical bug comments.

"You can go if you want," Ethan says suddenly. "Like, if you'd rather wait in the car, I get it."

I peer up at him. His expression is perfectly composed, but his jaw is slightly clenched. His brown eyes—the exact color of melted dark chocolate—are clear. From here, I can see the faint sprinkles of silver in them. "Do you want me to give you some time alone?" I ask.

He waits a beat. "I'd be happy if you stayed."

I nod and some inexplicable thread between us pulls the slightest bit. "I would, too."

His brow unfurrows, and I could swear something like relief flashes in his eyes. Part of me wants to keep watching him, wants to keep my gaze on the planes of his ever-changing face, but I look away.

We stand for a while in a peaceful, comfortable silence, and I'm happy just to be here with him. It's not like we even have to talk. Ethan and I can just... be.

Eventually, he takes a breath. "You ready?"

"Whenever you are."

He holds out a hand, gesturing for me to go first. I pass by him, but as I walk, he takes my wrist. His big hand practically encapsulates mine as he gently holds on. I look back at him, see a sadness as he glances at the gravestone once more.

"Val, I..." he starts, and his voice cracks.

Suddenly, that invisible thread between us tugs tight, and my arms are circling behind his neck as he wraps his around me. He pulls me against him.

It's the first hug we've shared in four years. My cheek still fits beneath his collarbone, and he curves his head down into my hair. It occurs to me that being locked in his arms like this feels like coming home after a long time spent away. I decide that it doesn't matter what this means, if it means anything at all. Maybe Ethan and I will always "just be" whatever we are.

He starts to pull away and I follow his lead. "Thanks. Guess I needed that."

"Seems like it." I smile. There's an intensity in the depths of his eyes that makes me a little breathless.

"Sounds like you needed today, too."

"How do you mean?"

"Sounds like you were short of sleep."

I sock him in the shoulder. Try to ignore the fact that my cheeks are burning fifty shades of red. "Yeah. Okay."

"Don't worry, Teeny." He chuckles. "It's cute. Your loud and unabashed snoring is one of my favorite things about you."

Please don't say stuff like that...

I suddenly feel altogether too close to him, and I take a step away. I shoot him a glare, but my mouth is betraying me, tugging up at the corners. "Okay, wise guy. Let's get on the road, shall we?"

"Absolutely. Have to get to the hotel."

"Two rooms, right?"

"Two rooms."

I breathe a secret sigh of relief. My own room far, far away from Ethan is exactly what I need right now. Because even though I vowed to put the past where it belongs on this trip, I'm presently feeling a lot of very familiar, very unwanted and unwarranted feelings

Friends! We're just friends, Val!

How quickly the heart seems to forget.

16

VAL

True to his word, Ethan *did* book us two rooms.

Right next to each other. Connected by an adjoining door.

I wish I could say that I wasn't hyper aware of every sound in the night, every creak and bump, but I was. Partly because I was wondering if he'd knock on my door (likely to ask for extra toilet paper or something sexy like that), and partly because I was worried my snoring would come back with a vengeance and he'd hear me through the walls.

But I fall into a heavy, dreamless sleep, and when I wake, the sunlight is streaming through the windows of the roadside hotel.

I lie in bed for a while, spread-eagled in my pajama shorts and old Top Gun T-shirt. It's full of holes around the bottom and one side is stretched out from a fitful, mildly violent sleep a couple summers ago when the A/C was out.

I check the time on my phone and sit straight up. Ethan's going to roast me for waking up past 9am. I'm shocked he didn't wake me himself.

I'm momentarily distracted by a calendar reminder on my screen—something from the Brookrose. I feel a twinge of guilt for ditching Ivy this weekend, and make a split second decision to call her. It doesn't even occur to me that calling the Brookrose has the bonus advantage of delaying another heart-confused day in the vicinity of Ethan Holmes.

Nope. Not at all.

"Brookrose Inn, Ivy speaking," a cheery voice answers.

"Hey, it's Val. Thought I'd call and see how you're doing?"

"Val!" Ivy screeches so loud, I have to hold the phone away from my ear. "How's the trip? Doing some fun stuff so far? You better not be worrying about how things are going here. That's *not* the right way to adventure."

Ivy continues to scold me and I hold back a giggle. "No... well, yes actually. I wanted to make sure you're doing okay."

"Totally fine, everything's under control."

I'm sure it is. Over the last week, I've seen how Ivy works. She's calm and patient, has this incredible confidence... because she literally knows *everything*. The woman is on top of every detail, is aware of every single thing that's happening around the Inn. How she manages to stay on the ball is beyond impressive.

"Happy to hear it," I say with a smile. "But honestly, let me know if you need me and I'll get Ethan to drive me back in a heartbeat."

"Don't even think about it. Now, enough about me, tell me about the road trip! I'm basically a twenty-three-year-old grandma, let me live vicariously through you."

I give her a rundown of everything that's been going on. I tell her about how surprisingly fun the paintball game was, and how I almost died via spider. I tell her about my horrendous snoring in the car, and the sobering moment we stopped at the cemetery.

The one thing I don't tell her about are the alleged "sparks."

"That sounds awesome, Val. I bet Ethan's glad to have you along for the ride."

I pick at a hole in my shirt. "I hope so. I'm glad I came. Feels like a nice way to honor his granddad."

"That's great. Though I was wondering—" she cuts herself off. "No, never mind."

I frown, stop my fiddling. "What?"

"It's nothing. I don't want to overstep."

Now worried that this is work related and she actually *does* need me back, I press on. "Seriously, Ivy. What is it?"

"Well... has anything ever..." When she speaks again, her voice is almost a whisper. "*Happened* with you two?"

Oh. Wasn't expecting that.

My mind goes into shock/panic mode... AKA I start laughing like a maniacal Disney movie character. Goodness knows why that's my gut reaction.

"Hahaha!" I laugh away for about a year. "What makes you say that?"

"A few things." Ivy doesn't sound convinced by my incessant cackling. "I swear I saw something between you two."

"Like what?" I ask before I can think it, before I can mask the raw curiosity in my voice.

"Like... you seemed different around him, more relaxed. And he couldn't keep his eyes off you the entire time we were talking."

I press my hand to my cheeks in an effort to cool them down. "No way. We were only all together for, like, five minutes, and for most of those minutes, he was talking to me anyway."

Ugh. Why do I sound like a teenager talking to her best friend about her crush?

"Whatever you say." Ivy's voice has this smug, knowing note to it that is completely uncalled for. "I thought there was something between you two, but clearly I'm off my rocker."

She laughs and I cough out a half-hearted chuckle. Something is swirling deep inside me, rising up from my stomach and making my heart race. I shoot to a stand and start pacing around the room. "No, nothing. I mean, we dated for a bit in high school, but that's long over now. And besides, everything with Randal is so fresh. I just want to be single..."

I trail off. Don't hear Ivy's response.

Because my pacing has taken me to a window overlooking the parking lot of the hotel and I've spotted a very toned, very shirtless Ethan placing a duffel bag into the car.

My logical brain knows that I should look away, but I physically can't. My eyes devour his muscular arms like they've been starved. The tight ropes of muscle in his back shift as he adjusts the bag, showing off the two dimples peeking up from above his black athletic shorts. His skin glistens in the morning sunlight—he must've just come back from a run.

As he turns back to grab another bag, he runs his hand through that thick hair of his, and the sight of his bicep popping almost makes me topple over.

"Val?"

I swallow thickly. *Heaven help me.*

"Val!"

"Wha—?" I ask, finally registering that A) I'm holding a phone, and B) I'm talking to Ivy on it.

"Did I lose you?"

"Sorry, no. Still here."

"I was asking how long you and Ethan have known each other?"

"Since we were kids." I'm still staring at him. "We basically grew up together."

"That's sweet. I love childhood friends."

I smile. "Yeah. I'm happy we're friends again."

At that moment, Ethan looks up at my window. He gives me a strange look, and holds up a hand in a hesitant wave. I wave back, still smiling away. Only then do I realize that he doesn't know I'm on the phone. So it looks like I've been staring out the window and smirking while he walks around shirtless.

Cheeks burning, I slink back so he can't see me anymore. I cannot be feeling this way, I can't go back to thinking Ethan's attractive. We all know where that led last time, and New Val doesn't go backwards. She only marches onwards.

Besides, he surely isn't feeling the same way about me. I may be working hard on my confidence, but anybody can see that Ethan's out of my league. It's an objective fact that I am completely comfortable with.

"I should let you go," Ivy says. "I'm sure you have another fun day planned."

I take in Ethan's perfectly defined abs, slightly mesmerized.

"It's definitely gonna be... something."

17

VAL

Four Years Ago

Ethan has something big planned for tonight. He keeps giving me shifty eyes and long glances, and I can feel it... something's coming.

"What?" I ask as I catch him looking at me again. We're in the backyard of his grandparents' house, spread out on a couple of blankets. I just got off the phone with my friend Megan about her crush on Noah Jackson. To be fair, every girl in our grade likes Noah Jackson. Except his best friend Dee. And me, of course.

I'm finally almost finished with my chapter, but my focus is completely on Ethan. Maybe because his focus is clearly so completely on me.

"Nothing." He turns away, squints against the sunlight. "Thinking about how cute you are when you're reading."

I flush a little. "Nuh, uh," I say, oh-so-modestly.

"Yeah, you get all frowny and your lips move with the words when you're really into the story."

"Look at you, stalker."

Ethan laughs, wraps an arm lazily over my waist. "Maybe I'm bored."

"You need a book."

"Or we could talk."

After a moment of true deliberation, I sigh heavily like I'm annoyed, put in my bookmark, and place my book next to me. Lie down so my side presses against his, and I interlace my arm with his. "Okayyyy. What do you want to talk about?"

"I don't know... Why is the sky blue?"

"Now *that's* boring." I giggle. "How about if we talk about what you have planned for tonight."

Ethan stiffens. "Next question."

"Okay. What about... why you kissed me that day?"

He looks at me and his chocolate eyes glow. "Which day?"

"The first time," I say, almost shyly. We've never talked about this before, but I've been curious. "On the last day of Junior year."

"Uhm, pretty sure you kissed *me*."

"Did not. That was all you."

Ethan frowns for a long moment. "Was it?" Then, before I can spiral into wondering if my memory's failing me, he shoots me a wink. "I just... felt like it."

I wait for him to say something more, maybe elaborate on the ever-growing mystery that is the thought process of a sixteen-year-old boy. But he doesn't.

I'm not expecting some grandiose declaration of love à la Romeo and Juliet. I don't even want him to hang off a ferris wheel like in *The Notebook* (seriously, that was far too dangerous a stunt in my books). But *something* would be nice, some hint as to what eventually won him over...

"Whatcha thinking about?" Ethan asks.

I smile. Why would I ruin such a nice moment by

bringing up things that don't matter? "Nothing much, just that I should get home soon." I slowly rise to a stand. "Alicia and Carmen should have settled their fight by now, and Mom might need some help around the house."

"Okay," Ethan stands next to me, brushes off his shorts. "I'll pick you up later?"

"Actually, I'll walk over. Knowing my parents, they'll want to chat with you for an hour and I'm assuming you have an entire evening carefully planned out..."

I wait, hoping this might illicit some hint about what to expect for tonight. All Ethan gives me is a nod.

I rise on my tiptoes to brush my lips against his. "7pm, right?"

"7pm. Get ready to be impressed with my newfound stick shift driving skills."

I pause. "I hope we're not going far."

"Don't worry, it's a short drive." Ethan laughs.

"Good." I wink at him, then turn to leave the yard. "See you later."

"Later, Teeny."

18

ETHAN

You know that vibrating sort of excited that kids get when they're on their way to an amusement park and are about to fill up on a thousand grams of sugar and adrenaline?

Yeah, that's Val right now. Multiplied by a hundred.

"Don't hurt yourself." I chuckle as she bounces around the passenger seat.

Her hands grasp her bare thighs, knuckles almost white. She turns to me and her expression makes me smirk. "You should've thought of that before telling me where we were going!"

"You're right. I should've anticipated you practically falling out of the truck every time we stop."

"You should have," Val agrees. "You *know* how excited I get about Tumbling Waters."

The name makes it sound a whole lot more dreamy and romantic than it is. Which is essentially one huge, flat swatch of farmland (cows included) dotted with towering water slides built in the 80s.

Val and I used to spend hours there, racing down the slides with our goggles and arm floaties. We'd splash around in the artificially colored, chlorine-scented pool (now horrifying to consider), and eat so many popsicles our teeth would turn red and our stomachs would ache (the thought of them still makes me queasy).

As we turn the corner, all of the park's glory comes into view. I spot the pile of tubes along the side fencing, the Monster Slide rising above the trees. The formerly crisp rainbow of water slides are now more of a sickly pastel hue after years of sun exposure.

I hope the safety standards have fared better…

"EEEEE!" Val squeals, placing both hands on the passenger window. "We're here!"

As soon as I park the car, Val's out the door. She bounces on her heels, putting on her sunglasses so she can stare at the park in awe. I sit for a moment, watching her. Nothing makes me happier than seeing Val smile like that.

She used to smile at me like that. I miss it. Miss her.

It's part of the reason why I've decided to go slightly beyond Pops's request for today. Spending all this time with Val has made me realize that I can't let this opportunity slip through my fingers. We may be older now, but Val is still the person I loved all those years ago, and her effect on me is the same.

It's made me wonder if I *could* do things differently. Be the one who fights for her. I want to prove to her that I deserve another chance. Show her that losing her the first time was the biggest mistake of my life, and now that I have her at my side again, I never want to let her go.

"You coming or what?" Val calls. She's staring impatiently at the truck and tapping her foot like she's a cartoon character. "I'll go in without you, don't think I won't!"

I make a show of rolling my eyes at her and get out of the car, grabbing the plastic bag I stuffed my swim trunks into. "Hold your horses, Teeny."

"They are held, but barely."

"And you say *I* make bad jokes."

She's still tapping her foot. "So, what's the task we have to complete here? I'm assuming we have to go on the water slides?"

"Actually, no. Pops only requested that we get ice cream."

"What?" Val raises her sunglasses so I get the full force of her flat gaze. "Let me get this straight. Pops wanted me to play *paintball*—which I have never done in my life—but didn't want us to go on the water slides where we spent our childhood?!"

She sounds so indignant that I have to chuckle. "Correct."

"Oh, Alfie." She sighs dramatically and I picture the little smile Pops used to have when he was particularly feisty. "But we're going anyway, right?"

"Of course we are. We're not coming to Tumbling Waters and not going on the slides. That would be lunacy."

She lifts a brow. "Good to see that your time away hasn't completely changed you."

I let my eyes meet hers. "Some things never change, Teeny."

Val's expression shifts, just slightly. Her mouth puckers at the corners, and she quickly looks away. "Why don't you go ahead into the park? I'll head to the shop and buy a swimsuit and meet you on the other side."

"I'll come with you."

To be clear, I'm *not* the kind of guy who normally likes shopping for clothes, but I want to spend every minute I can with her. Even if it means having to stand crammed amongst rows of clothes in a shop that smells of dust and plastic and is lit by those horrible fluorescent bulbs.

Val's smile falters. "You want to come with me to get a swimsuit?"

"If you want me to."

"Okay, like... you really don't have to. You should probably go ahead."

I peer at her, trying to guess what she's thinking. I decide to leave it up to her. "I'd like to spend time with you. But whatever you want, Teeny."

Her eyebrows lift like she's surprised by my response. She screws up her face in thought. "I guess you can come," she says slowly.

It's not the most enthusiastic response I've ever heard, but I'll take it.

We walk into the shop next to the park's entrance and Val goes to the bikini section. And it finally hits me that this might've been a mistake. Because the thought of Val trying on bikinis—that cute lace one, the high-waisted pink one, the multi-color one with the ties at the sides...

Heat gathers in my stomach and I decide to exit the area STAT. I head to the obligatory Boyfriend Seating Area next to the change rooms and grab a magazine. Try very, very hard not to think of Val in that white string bikini she's currently considering.

I've forced myself to be engrossed in an article about growing pears in California (thrilling), when Val walks up holding an assortment of bathing suits.

"I'm, uh... going to try these," she says.

"You sound unsure about that."

Val shrugs and looks at the change room but doesn't go in.

I scan her face. "What's wrong?"

"Nothing." She clears her throat, absentmindedly fingers the knot at the bottom of her oversized white T-shirt. "I'm just... I haven't worn a bathing suit in awhile."

"And this is a problem because...?"

She opens her mouth, seems to want to say something, but then thinks better of it. "I don't know. It feels, like, embarrassing or something."

"Embarrassing how?"

Val shrugs, but her gaze stays on the change room. All at once, I clue in to what she might be thinking... a thought process which is absolutely ridiculous and I intend to let her know. I place my hand firmly on hers. "Val, there's no reason for you to feel embarrassed. Literally *no reason*."

Her cheeks start to turn pink again. "No, that's okay. You don't have to say that."

"I'm not," I say, seriously blown away that she could ever feel this way. "This isn't, like, me being nice or anything. Trust me, I'm not that nice."

Val snorts, but she won't meet my gaze.

"Come on. Didn't you see the guy at the counter checking you out when we walked in?"

Now, she looks at me full on. "He did not."

"He did." My voice has dropped a couple octaves, sounds almost growly. *Careful, Ethan, or you'll give away how much that bothered you.* "The point is, you're hard on yourself, Teeny, but you shouldn't be. *Really* shouldn't be."

Val's still looking away and I have to repress the urge to tuck her hair behind her ear, run my fingers along the soft skin of her arms to reassure her. She swallows, finally meeting my eyes, and in those amber depths, there's a wariness. Like she doesn't believe me.

"You're gorgeous," I say, meaning every word. "You should see you how I see you."

Val holds my gaze for a long moment. She's testing me, and I don't intend to fail. Don't intend to let her down this time.

Something happens then—her expression clears and she

smiles. She leans towards me slightly, so her hip presses into me. Before I can react, she pulls away and walks to the change room. "Okay, okay. I'll try these on. No need to badger me about it."

The tension of the moment breaks and I chuckle. "I'm here whenever you're ready."

○ ○

In the end, Val chooses a high-waisted, slide-practical orange bikini that I already know will look fantastic on her. She goes to the front counter while I hang back, strolling around the shop while also subtly sizing up the worker.

He looks to be about our age, and is actually the shop manager, according to his nametag and his whole polo-shirt-and-pressed-khaki combo. He has shaggy black hair, a clean-cut appearance, and the kind of confidence that comes from knowing women find him attractive.

It doesn't bother me to think of him flirting with Val. Not at all.

"Find everything you need today?" He places his hands on the counter, obviously flexing his triceps.

"Yup, everything was great." Then, because she's Val and she befriends everyone, she adds, "I forgot my swimsuit."

"That's what we're here for." His eyes don't leave hers, and he crosses his arms casually. "You know, my dad owns Tumbling Waters."

"Really?"

"Uh-huh. And it's gonna fall to me someday. So, you know, I can probably get you in for free in a few years."

Subtle.

I refrain from rolling my eyes, remind myself that Val is

perfectly free and single to date whoever she wants. Or to not date at all. But hey, got to respect the chops of this guy.

I stare at some goggles on display with a new fervor, but I can still hear their conversation.

"That's awfully nice of you to offer."

"Yeah," he says. "It's a cool spot. Have you been before?"

"I used to come all the time growing up. I'm actually here for a little trip down memory lane with..."

At this point, I can't help but look over. Val is holding a hand towards me in a half-gesture. She doesn't elaborate.

It takes a second for the guy to size me up and the flirty smile drops off his face. He averts his gaze quickly. "Uh, right. Okay. Well, that'll be—"

"Hang on," Val interrupts. "Did you want something, Ethan? Maybe those kids goggles you're staring at?"

Huh?

Oh, fantastic. In my attempt at nonchalance, I picked up a box of sparkly pink goggles and am cradling them close to my chest. I press my lips together, shove them back onto the shelf. "No, I'm good."

"You sure? No goggles, or arm floaties, or maybe even a —Ooooh!" She suddenly lunges forward and picks up a glaringly bright sweater. "This looks *exactly* like a sweater I used to have!"

The faded edges of a memory come back to me as I stare at the blinding piece of fabric. "You had a tie-dye sweatshirt?"

"Yeah, when I was, like, 7. Mom got it for Alicia, but she didn't want it and it didn't fit Carmen so it came to me."

"Do you want it, Teeny?"

She frowns, even as she holds the sweater to her chest lovingly. "Tie-dye isn't really my color."

"Sure it is. It's literally every color."

"You know what I mean." She puts the sweater back. "I shouldn't. I'm a grownup now. I should be wearing suits and fancy professional clothes."

I raise a brow. "You can't wear a suit 24/7, Teeny. Even the most put-together people wear sweats sometimes."

Val sighs while literally petting the sweater. She doesn't respond.

On a whim, I take the sweater and go to the guy at the counter. "I'll get this. And the swimsuit."

Val places a hand on my arm. "What're you—"

"I'm buying these. You want the sweater, I'm getting you the sweater."

She stares up at me while I swipe my card in the machine. "Ethan, you don't have to do that."

I take the bag and turn towards her. My gaze softens as I look at her wide, amber eyes, her pouting mouth that I've remembered kissing countless times. "I want to. Because you deserve every tie-dye sweater in the world if that's what you want. And I'm sorry if I ever made you feel otherwise."

19

VAL

I discovered something important today.

Spending the day at a water park as an adult is completely underrated.

After the initial discomfort of the whole "trying on bathing suits with Ethan sitting not five feet away" situation, we were off to the races.

Literally. We went down slides that twisted and turned around and on top of each other. We rode down the River Rider in multi-colored tubes. I'd put an arm out ahead of him to give him a late start, or he'd grab my ankle in the pool to slow me down. I watched (from a safe, comfortable distance) as he went down the Monster Slide.

I've never been brave enough to do the Monster Slide, and I don't see that changing anytime soon. I might aspire to be full of Girlboss bravery and energy, but it's baby steps to get there...

Maybe I'm just fooling myself.

"So what do you say? Time for one more?" I ask as I sit up from my sun lounger. Ethan and I claimed a couple by the pool at lunchtime and have been lazing around all afternoon in post-hot-dog-eating bliss. What is it about food from sketchy amusement park food stands that tastes *so* good?

Hmm. After watching a couple Netflix documentaries, maybe I shouldn't go looking for that answer.

Ethan lifts his head and opens literally half an eye. "Park's closing soon, everyone's heading out. We might be too late, Teeny."

"Well, with that attitude..." I joke, shoving his shoulder. My stomach drops out to feel his sun-kissed skin beneath my fingers, the taut muscles in his upper tricep. I retract my hand like I've been burned.

It's a shoulder. A SHOULDER!

Why on earth are man shoulders so sexy? Please, explain.

He frowns, oblivious to my inner conundrum. "Good point. Besides, you haven't had a chance to do the Monster Slide yet."

I shoot him a tired look. "Ha ha. You know where I stand with the Monster Slide and all of its way-too-steep, guaranteed-butt-burn glory."

"Come on, Teeny. Live a little."

Ethan says this with one eye in a winky-squint against the sunlight, his hands clasped behind his head so his biceps are popping out and looking particularly bicepy. I don't even think he's flexing.

He looks like a freaking, annoying Greek god again and I'm not enjoying the way my body's responding. Particularly the way my gaze is zeroing in on his smirk, his full bottom lip that looks just so bite-able...

Yup, I'm officially imagining what it might be like to "live a little" with Ethan again...

And it has nothing to do with the Monster Slide.

"Teeny?" he says.

"Yeah?"

"Do I have something on my face?"

I blink. "What?"

"You're staring at me." He brushes his fingers across his bottom lip—a move which should *not* make my insides do Olympic-gymnast level flips. "Do I have ketchup on my mouth?"

"Nope." I shake my head, at a loss for any sort of smooth transition out of the fact that I've been staring at him like the light spatter of freckles across his cheekbones could decode the secrets of the Bermuda Triangle.

"Good." He smiles, but then his gaze sharpens and he sits up abruptly. Faces me so his knees almost graze mine.

He's staring at *my* mouth now, his brown eyes locked on me as my senses are bathed in his firewood scent. Seriously, he should not smell so good after being in chlorine all day. He leans in close and I find myself leaning in, too.

What is happening right now? And why can't I bring myself to stop it?

"Stay still." He reaches towards me.

My breath catches.

"You've got sunscreen on your lip."

Oh. Of course. He's staring at me because *my face is literally dirty.*

"Do I?!" I paw at my mouth.

He chuckles at my frantic movements. After a beat, he shakes his head. "You're missing it." He puts out a hand again. "May I?"

I can't bring myself to respond, so I nod. He reaches out, places his big, rough palm on my cheek and warmth spreads from where he's touching me. His thumb slowly traces my upper lip, wiping away the traitor sunscreen. The feeling of his calloused skin on my mouth makes my heart-beat spike.

He retracts his hand slowly, leaving me weirdly breathless. He shifts slightly and I see the rise and fall of his chest, the way his eyes seem darker than ever.

"That's better," he says, but I could swear his voice is different. Deeper.

Snap out of it, Val!

"Anyway." My voice is shrill. "One more time on the slides?"

Ethan hops to his feet. "Monster Slide?"

His expression is now full of a challenge and I scrunch my nose, pretending that I'm considering it while really getting myself firmly back in order. "You go ahead. I'll do the River Rider once more."

"Come on, Teeny," he says, then goes so far as to give me that sweet, almost pleading gaze that used to melt my resolve like warm caramel sauce. "We can't leave without you trying it."

"I've never been on the Monster Slide. No need to change that now. Old dog, new tricks, all that jazz."

"You're so dramatic. You're far from being an old dog."

"If we lived in the time of my regency novels, I'd be an unwed spinster by now."

"Sexy." He chuckles. "Now I'm picturing the evil lady from *Pride and Prejudice*."

"Well, it's not quite like that," I say. "For one thing, she's played by the great Dame Judi Dench."

"And for another, she's not you. You'd still look gorgeous as an evil old lady."

His response catches me off guard. Is he serious? I never thought I'd be pleasantly surprised to be called a gorgeous old lady, but then again, I never thought I'd be back at Tumbling Waters with Ethan.

And what is with this calling me "gorgeous" all of a sudden? He's used that exact word twice today... But he must mean it like I'm one of those show cats who's back from the groomers.

"So you don't want to go?" Ethan asks.

I hesitate for a moment. Peek at the slide, and almost reconsider. Almost feel like I could do it and be the brave Val I aspire to be. But at the last moment, I chicken out. "No, I don't."

His lips twitch. "Teeny. I know your tell."

"I don't know what you're talking about. Now, I'll race you. Loser has to get the ice creams on the way out." I take a deep breath, then say in a rush, "On-your-mark-get-set-GO!"

Without giving him time to react, I start walk-jogging like a madwoman towards the slides. I understand why they have the no running rule… it just makes it so much harder when you're trying to compete with a six-foot-something man on a mission.

As expected, Ethan catches up to me within seconds. "Did you really think you'd get away with that?"

"Technically, I did get away with it. It's not my fault you have freakish giant legs."

"I think you quite like my giant legs."

I throw a glare over my shoulder. "And I think you're about to lose."

I glance around for any lurking workers, then pick up my speed. I'm not running… but I'm also not *not* running.

"Don't you know that's dangerous?" is all I hear before a pair of strong arms wrap around my waist and I'm lifted from the ground. My legs continue to kick out for a second before I freeze in shock.

Ethan unceremoniously tips me over his shoulder.

"Ethan!" I squawk. "What're you doing?!"

"I'm keeping the pool area safe for everyone." He pats the backs of my thighs. My cheeks flame red.

"This—I mean, really!" I sputter, infuriated. I whack my hands on his back. "Put me down!"

He doesn't answer. Just walks towards the slides, whistling away like he's carrying a pillow on his shoulder and not a full-grown woman. He even has the audacity to say hi to people passing us by, like this is totally normal. I have the pleasure of seeing the shocked, mildly concerned faces on the other side of his greeting.

"Put me down! Pops would not approve of this."

We've reached the base of the Monster Slide and Ethan lowers me to the ground with a surprising amount of gentleness for someone who just strolled around with a friend-nap victim over his shoulder. He smiles at me, and there's a flash of something tender in his eyes. "I think he would. If he knew you were endangering the pool attendees."

Dang it. He's probably right.

He holds an arm out and gestures up the slide. "Ladies first."

I'm about to protest, but he silences me with a look. Not a mean or harsh look, but a "you know you're going to do it anyway" kind of look.

I give him a long glare before turning away and climbing up the Monster Slide. I don't say another word to him, but he's right behind me the whole time, whistling like we're grocery shopping and not risking our lives.

As we climb higher, my anger turns into something a lot more primal and fear-based. Soon, I'm crawling—both due to the exertion, and due to the thought of being stuck on this metallic, creaky, ancient stairway to an even more terrifying slide.

Finally, it's too much.

"I don't think I can do this," I utter, slowing to an official stop. I hate how small my voice is.

Ethan stops, too. He doesn't usher me forward or push me, but he doesn't back down either. "Sure you can."

He says this with so much confidence, so much certainty. It makes me doubt his sanity and/or memory that he has this much faith in me. "You don't know what I'm capable of anymore."

He's silent for a moment, and I suddenly wonder if my words bothered him. When he speaks again, his voice is heavy. "It's been awhile Val, but I still know who you are, know how brave and strong you are. You can do anything you put your mind to."

Except stop thinking about your lips, apparently.

FOCUS, Val! This is neither the time, nor the place.

But actually, thinking about his lips is working for me...

Slowly, I start up again, remembering his lips when he smirked at me by the pool. Is that weird? Maybe. But credit where credit's due, I manage to climb the final two levels to the platform without stopping once.

"You did it!" Ethan exclaims when we reach the top.

I high-five him with no small amount of pride. I *did* do it! I'm one step closer to New Val.

"You made it," a flat voice says. The teenaged pool attendant is sitting in his chair, scrolling through his phone and bouncing his leg impatiently. "I've been waiting for ages. I thought maybe one of you was really old or injured or something." He dignifies us with a bored glance. "You *are* old, though."

Ethan raises an amused brow. "Thanks for waiting for us."

"Yeah, I mean you've got, like..." The worker checks his watch. "Three minutes and forty seconds."

"Not a second to lose then." Ethan walks towards the slide. "Shall we, Teeny?"

I step forward slowly and my entire being recoils to see

the height, the sheer steepness of the slide. It literally goes straight down, maybe even concaves towards the bottom. I was never good at math, but *surely* that angle is more than 180 degrees?!

"I just..." I stutter, my voice squeaky. Fear always turns me into one of those animated mice from *Cinderella*. "I don't think... I can't."

"You did the stairs, didn't you?" Ethan says reasonably. "You can do this, too."

"You can go down together if you need to. All of the really young and scared kids do that with their parents," the worker adds helpfully. Not. "Whatever floats your boat."

He doesn't seem to realize how perfectly apt that expression is given where we are, but Ethan catches my eye with a smirk. And suddenly, the thought of sliding down with him seems even more dangerous than going alone.

"What do you say, Teeny?"

I shift on my feet. "You should enjoy your last go. Who knows when you'll be back."

"Oh, I'll be back. I can't stay away too long."

I refrain from pointing out that, far as I'm aware, the last time he was here was four whole years ago.

"Chop chop, y'all," the worker chimes in.

"Fine, let's do it." I clasp my hands together. "So how should we... how do we...?"

"You get in the slide first, and I'll sit behind you."

I follow Ethan's instructions, sitting with my legs out in front of me in the cool water. Goosebumps race up my body and I realize how cold I am now that it's the end of the day.

But the chill doesn't last long, because soon, Ethan's chest is pressed against my back and his legs are stretching out on either side of mine. There is so much contact, so much bare skin to skin that I stiffen automatically. I'm the filling in an Ethan taco and I don't hate it. Not one bit.

I barely register what's happening past the feeling of him against me. But suddenly, we're moving forward, Ethan's strong legs pressing against mine...

And then, we're sliding.

And I'm screaming bloody murder while the slide drops away beneath me. Ethan and I hurtle into thin air and I grasp for his hands around my waist, clawing at him.

After what feels like an eternity of terrifying, heart-wrenching freefall, the ground catches us again and we're shooting forward along the base of the slide. I'm still screaming, but silently because I have no breath left.

We come to a stop, and I'm frozen. My heart bangs against my ribcage and my blood pounds out a beat that could rival any rock n' roll drum solo.

Eventually, I hear it. Hear the laughter.

Ethan is cracking up. Cackling away behind me. His chest shakes and his abs flex against the base of my spine. I sit straight as a board and turn to face him, chock-full of... anger, or laughter, or fear, or delirium. Maybe all of the above.

"What?" I basically shout.

He continues to laugh, his hands still clasped loosely around my waist. "You screamed yourself hoarse."

"I almost died!" I shout again. We're going the anger route, apparently.

"You didn't," he says. "I was with you the whole time. I would never let you go, Teeny."

There's that tenderness again, a vulnerability and softness that sends me spiraling. His wet hair hangs over his forehead and his lips are slightly parted. His chocolate eyes are filled with sincerity as they meet mine.

Suddenly, my anger evaporates and is replaced by a sudden, almost desperate need to be closer to him.

My body's a livewire on high voltage, every nerve crackling with electricity. It's all I can do to fight it, not to give into the urge to fall back into him. To have his lips on mine and have him kiss me in the hungry, heady way he used to...

Then, I notice something. Ethan's stopped laughing, too. His eyes are dark pits, and his grip around my waist tightens the slightest bit. His gaze drops to my lips for a heartbeat, and he lightly bites his bottom lip.

Oh, my gosh.

Ethan Holmes wants to kiss me.

This is all I need for my restraint to fly right out the window.

Ethan and I move in tandem, like some unconscious dance. His big hands spread around my waist and pull me towards him. I'm leaning in closer, my hands grasping his shoulders.

We're so close now, a breath away, and—

"Park's closed!!"

The voice tears through the air, bursting our bubble.

"We're closing, guys," the attendant shouts again. "Time to go."

Ethan blinks, his jaw clenching as he gets out of the slide. He holds a hand towards me, and I take it. This time, I don't ignore the sparks that travel through my body and leave a fire in their wake.

This time, I wonder if he's feeling them, too.

20

ETHAN

I'm in Pops's pickup, trying to focus on the road, but my world is consumed by Val.

I'm aware of the way she bites her nails in my peripheral vision, how she shifts to tuck her legs beneath her. All I can think about is the memory of her soft, smooth skin against me—her legs pressed within mine, her hips against my thighs, her back on my chest. Her fingers grasping for my hands locked around her.

Her pomegranate shampoo is filling the truck. I remember the way her gaze dropped to my lips when we reached the end of the slide...

I make a decision. Signal and turn off the road. Park the car. Val looks at me with wide eyes as I pull her towards me. Her fingers tangle into my hair, holding on tight as our bodies crash together.

And finally, *finally*, I feel her soft lips against mine—

"So where are we off to?"

The question wrenches me back to the present like an electric jolt applied to my spine.

Frick, Ethan! Where were you going with that exactly?!

I clear my throat, turn to look at the very real and non-daydream Val sitting in the passenger seat as we drive away from Tumbling Waters. Although she looks even better in real life than she does in my imagination. How does she manage that? It's like my mind can't capture every little, intricate, beautiful thing about her.

"Ethan?" she asks, seeming almost nervous. "Everything okay?"

"Yeah, 'course." I clear my throat again. "Sorry, was trying to remember the way to Billy's Diner."

"Oh. Good. We're going there for dinner?"

"Milkshakes. Pops clearly didn't consider that we might not want milkshakes directly after ice cream at the water park. But seeing as we missed out on ice cream and I'm starving, I could really go for one of those onion ring burgers."

"Ugh, those are *rank*." Val scrunches her adorable nose. "I'm getting one, too."

I chuckle, happy that Val has relaxed. I understand why she was nervous before—she was worried I was going to bring up what almost happened at the base of the slide.

Because it did almost happen, right? Val almost leaned in to kiss me; I was definitely leaning in to kiss her...

And now here we are, speeding towards our final destination for the day. We've been sitting in silence while my brain vacillates dizzily between wanting to bring up the almost kiss and risk overstepping, and (apparently) daydreaming inappropriate things.

"Ooh, this is a good one." Val reaches for the volume dial on the radio, but right before she touches it, she freezes. "Is it okay if I turn it up?"

"Of course, Teeny." I give her a look. "You don't have to ask."

"Figured I would. Being polite and all that."

"You don't have to be polite around me. You don't have to be anything."

"Oh. Thanks." She shoots me a quick, shy smile.

Val turns up the volume and it's *Living on a Prayer* by Bon Jovi. Basically the anthem of our teen years. To my surprise and delight, Val starts to hum along quietly. Soon, she gains confidence and the humming turns into singing which turns into a full karaoke-style rock out. She belts the song, her voice slightly off-key. I chuckle, shooting amused glances her way.

"You're not going to sing with me?" she asks during a break in the verse.

"I'm not sure you want me to. You remember how tone deaf I am."

"Don't be boring, Ethan." She shoots me a wink, all bravado.

I hold her gaze for a heartbeat, then decide to take her up on the challenge. I join in, belting out the words in a way that I've only done in recent years when I was alone in the car or in the shower. We're a sorry pair, singing along terribly off-key. Bon Jovi would probably crucify us if he heard this version of his song.

For a heady moment though, as the song crescendoes—with the windows down, the sun shining into the car, and Val's curly hair blowing against my arm—I feel really, genuinely happy.

"Can I ask you a question?" I ask when the song comes to an end.

Val turns down the volume. It's an ad now, and I almost miss her singing voice.

Ugh, I'm such a sap.

"Shoot," Val says lightly, but I hear the uncertainty in her voice.

"How do you feel about second chances?"

"Second chances for what exactly? Like giving that beef stew that gave me food poisoning for three days in junior year another try? Or like forgiving Alicia for taking the last Cherry Laffy Taffy when we were six?"

"Hmm. Closer to the second one."

I feel rather than see Val's smile. "I guess you could say I would be... open to forgiving Alicia."

"Really?" I give Val a look. "You think you could do it?"

She's quiet for a long moment. "Forgiveness is... complicated. I feel like it shifts, moves, is almost a living thing. If you want to have an ongoing relationship with someone—as I do with Alicia, most of the time—the ability to forgive is key. People hurt people, it's a fact of life. Forgiveness is what you do with that hurt."

"You're wise for your age," I say, using her expression.

"It's something I learned in recent months. Since Randal broke up with me."

"This was in your self-discovery books?"

Val shoots me a look. "You've been listening."

"I always listen. You just assume I'm not paying attention."

She chuckles. "I tried a few different things after we ended—ate chocolate ice cream and binged romcoms; got on a dating app for half a second, then realized it wasn't for me..."

I smirk, mildly curious about what Val's profile on a dating app might've looked like. "Ah, the things you do to get over someone."

"What do you do?"

Val's voice is unexpectedly weighted. I decide to be honest. "I've only had my heart broken once, and I was a complete and total wreck. Almost went and got myself a bad haircut with crazy bangs or whatever."

She giggles, shifts slightly in her seat. "Ooh, I forgot

about that one. I'll have to tell Ivy so she can add that to her list." She doesn't expand further on what this list is, but maybe it's best I don't know. "Anyway, none of that was really helping, so I started reading articles online. And from there, I came across all of these books and that's where I learned about forgiveness. Not only forgiving him, but also forgiving myself."

"Forgiving yourself? For what?"

"Oh, for so many things. I did so many things wrong, Ethan. Starting with the fact that I got together with Randal so soon after things ended with you. It wasn't fair to him, but I was lost and confused and hurt. He made me feel like everything could be okay again."

I nod, my heart heavy. "I'm so sorry, Val. I'm sorry I ever hurt you like that."

"Don't hold it against yourself. Forgiveness, remember?"

"Well, I do want you in my life going forward. So yes, forgiveness is all I can ask for."

Val is silent again. Then, she says, "You're already forgiven, but thank you for apologizing."

And just like that, I've finally told her that I'm sorry after years of feeling it and knowing it and being consumed by it. Finally, she heard the words, and believed them.

"Enough with all this seriousness," she says. "Where's fun Ethan? I need him back."

"I'm pretty sure fun Ethan only lives around you. Most of the time, I'm serious, responsible Ethan."

"Well, serious, responsible Ethan needs to take a chill pill. *You're on vacation*," Val says in a droney, nasally voice that makes me snort with laughter.

"Oh, I do have one fun thing to tell you," I say with a smile. "I'm in the final round for a sous-chef position in a fine dining restaurant in Montana."

"Of course you would think that a job offer would count as 'fun.'"

I give her a look. "Okay, how's this: it's a fine dining restaurant *on a train car*."

Val's eyebrows pop up. "That ups the 'fun' factor a little."

I laugh.

"So you'd be a fancy chef on a fancy train?"

"Basically. But don't get too excited, I haven't been offered the job yet." Then, without thinking, I add, "And even if I am, I'm not sure I'm going to take it."

"What's stopping you?"

"I..." I frown. "I don't know if I want to be a chef."

Val's eyes widen, as do mine. I'm as surprised as she is by my revelation. She just makes me feel so comfortable, like I can tell her anything. The words slipped out.

"Oh. Well, that is a pickle." She sits back, her brow crinkled. "You know, I never saw you as a chef. I pictured you as more of, like, a baker. Making cakes and sweets."

"A baker..." I repeat, remembering vividly how much I loved baking with my grandma. I never seriously considered any other option than being a chef. It made sense—financially, personally, practically—that I would go down that road. "There was this cafe I used to love in Aston Falls called Morning Bell. They had the *best* scones, the cheese ones especially."

"Exactly. You always seemed so passionate about baking. And you're so good at it. Heck, you could open a bakery with your brownies *alone*."

I screw up my face. "I don't think I'd want to have my own bakery."

"Why not?"

"I don't know. Running a bakery sounds like a lot of management and paperwork. And suits."

She shrugs. "Well you'd have a loyal customer in me. I will go broke buying your brownies."

"Don't be crazy, Teeny." I give her a wink. "You'd get a friends and family discount."

"Har dee har har."

But she's laughing, the sound bubbly and light, and soon, I'm joining in. My mind is racing with possibilities and questions I've never truly allowed myself to consider, but for now, I'm happy to be laughing with Val as we head towards a run-down diner with—admittedly—the best burgers I've ever had.

A comfortable silence settles between us and Val smiles as she gazes out towards the fields and mountains. The sunlight makes her skin glow.

"I missed this," she murmurs, almost too quietly for me to hear.

I match her tone, speak from the heart. "I missed you."

—

21

VAL

"VAL!" Ivy sings into the phone. "How are you, old chap?!"

"Old chap?" I ask with a giggle. "I'm flattered."

"Trust me, it's a highly complimentary greeting. I've been binging Fawlty Towers lately and it's put me in quite a posh mood." There's the sound of rustling papers on her end. "So, what's up? I hope you're not calling about work again."

I shift on the bed in my hotel room, pulling a pillow across my lap. Ethan and I got back from Billy's not long ago, and I doubt I'll be moving much more tonight. The burger was better than I remembered, and I ended up finishing the entire, towering stack. If I'd taken another bite, Ethan would've had to roll me out of the restaurant.

Meanwhile, he put his burger away like it was a light salad. Guess he needs the protein to build those incredible triceps of his.

Sigh. Even the thought of his shoulders gets me all dreamy-eyed.

"I'm not checking in about work, I swear." She doesn't need to know that I'm crossing my fingers. "I, uh... wanted to say that I have another post-breakup activity to add to the list!"

"Ooh!" hollers a voice that isn't Ivy's.

"Ouch, Dais," Ivy grumbles. "You can't scream into people's ears like that."

"Sorry, sorry. But can you blame me? I just walked into the most interesting conversation." There's a light scuffle, and then the other woman speaks clearly. "Val, right? I'm Daisy Griffiths, I don't know if you remember me."

I chuckle. Mirror Valley is a small town, we don't usually do or require introductions, but I appreciate that Daisy gave me her name. It erases any potential first name awkwardness. "Hey Daisy, of course I remember you. I went to school with Dee."

"Ah, my sweet, annoying baby sister." Daisy chuckles. "But I'm obsessed with this conversation you two are having. Ivy here incorrectly assumed the lobby was empty at this hour and put you on speakerphone."

"It's not my fault you happened to show up after finishing your dead lifts or whatever it is you do at the gym."

"Work at the front desk, dumb-dumb, just like you do," Daisy teases. "If we're talking about breakups though, I take it you're on the dating scene as well, Val?"

I screw up my mouth. "I'm... not sure. My boyfriend Randal and I broke up a few months ago and I've been on a single streak since then."

"Bu-ut," Ivy sings. "She happens to be on a road trip right now, and not alone. Do you remember Ethan Holmes from school?"

"He was in Dee's grade too, right? Didn't he used to hang out with Noah?"

"Noah was his gym buddy," I volunteer for some reason. "Ethan and I were best friends back then."

"OOH!" Daisy crows. "I *love* a good friends-to-more

kinda story! And besides, you two are clearly meant to be, Van."

So much for avoiding first name awkwardness. "It's Val, actually."

"No, *Van*," Daisy says again with more passion. "Your couple name."

"Our what?"

"You've never heard of couple names? Well, you two are clearly meant to be because Val plus Ethan combines to make Van. Well, Vathan, actually, but that's not as catchy. *And* you two are on a road trip. See? Perfect."

I stifle a laugh. It's some whacked out reasoning, but I appreciate Daisy's enthusiasm.

"That's ridiculous and you know it." Ivy sighs. "Couple names mean nothing."

"You wait 'til you meet a swoony guy whose name matches with yours. Val, what did you say your ex's name was?"

"Randal."

"Oh. Oh no, that's no good. No one wants to be a '*Vandal*.'"

"Daisss!" Ivy groans.

"Okay, okay. So, tell us what's happening with this hottie nomadic friend of yours."

"He's none of those things." I chuckle. "Okay, he's not nomadic, but I guess the rest is pretty accurate." Heat rises to my cheeks and I fiddle with the purple pillow tassel as I remember being pressed against Ethan at the water park. The moment I saw something I could only describe as fire in his eyes.

He wanted to kiss me, I know he did. I'm just not sure how I'm supposed to feel about that.

"So..." Ivy says. "You like him?"

"What? No." I shake my head adamantly. "I can't like him. I can't fall for him after everything that happened between us and the way he ended things."

The heart may quickly forgive and forget, but the mind is another story.

"Just because you can't fall for him doesn't mean you won't," Daisy says with a surprising amount of heaviness. For a moment, I wonder if she's speaking from experience, but then, she giggles. "He sounds like a fun, adventurous guy if he enjoys road trips."

"He is." I smile. "And he's a genuinely good person. When I'm with him, I feel safe. Comfortable. You know?"

"I missed you."

That's what he said in the truck before the diner. And the way he said the words so seriously, like they'd been on his mind for a while. But how can he say these things—and say that he wants me in his life going forward—while also telling me about this job on a fancy train car? Mirror Valley may have restaurants, but only the kind that smell of delicious fried foods and welcome cowboy boots and jean jackets. Not a fine dining establishment in sight.

The reality is that all good things come to an end, and this road trip is one of them. We both know why we broke up all those years ago; there's no sense in having history repeat itself.

"Anyway, it doesn't matter." I clear my throat. "He's got this exciting opportunity in Montana, so he's headed back soon and everything will be back to normal."

Even as I speak though, I feel a small, totally unreasonable seed of hope planting deep in my stomach. A hope that this could be more than just a weekend road trip reunion for Ethan and me. That we could do things differently this time around.

See? Unreasonable.

"Whenever you're ready, you should come along with me to some of the singles events in Mirror Valley," Daisy chirps. "They're... well, I wouldn't recommend going to actually *find* someone, but it's pretty entertaining to watch people pair up and split up. Like our very own *Bachelor in Paradise.*"

"I'll bring the popcorn." I smile. "Now I'm going to be boring and ask about work. Ivy, how're things?"

"It's been great! I had an idea yesterday when I was at the hair salon. I was leafing through this wedding magazine and had an idea that maybe the Brookrose could look into hosting weddings. I've added that to my to-do list to look into. And then..."

Knock knock.

The sound startles me and I look at the door that adjoins to Ethan's room.

A sheet of paper slides beneath it.

While Ivy goes on about work, I roll myself (literally) off the bed and walk across the floor (because no matter how cute this hotel is, the dark maroon carpet should probably remain a roll-free zone).

I pick up the paper and scan the writing. It's like the letters we used to leave in the letter box...

Roses are red, violets are blue

I feel like an idiot writing this, but I'd like to picnic with you.

Tomorrow at the park,

We'll get an early start.

My heart warms as I imagine Ethan rolling his eyes at his own note. He's such a reluctant sap; it cracks me up. Or it used to, when he did stuff like this for me all the time. Sweet stuff, like invite me to a picnic in the park...

That seed of hope blooms freely again. It's almost like Ethan's strategizing this—blasting down each and every one of my walls, all of my reservations, in a calculated attack.

And with every word, every heated look, every stupid, cheesy note, my feelings are getting harder to ignore.

22

VAL

Four Years Ago

I tease my fingers through my hair once more, but it already looks pretty wild and voluminous. I was going to straighten it, but thought twice. Ethan always calls me beautiful, but I've seen the look in his eyes when I wear my hair down and curly.

That look alone could power entire cities.

I check my reflection, smooth down my blue dress with the cap sleeves that hugs my body (and floats away from it) just right. I found it in a vintage shop with Mom a few months back and have been waiting for the right occasion to wear it.

After a final spin in the mirror, I grab my purse, slip into my wedge sandals, say bye to Mom and Dad, and launch out the door. It's a gorgeous summer evening, and the setting sun casts a golden hue across our neighborhood. Birds sing in the trees, and the smell of smokey barbecue makes my stomach grumble. There's a mugginess in the air that means rain is coming, but for now, everything's perfect.

I practically skip to Ethan's grandparents' house,

bursting with excitement. When I get there, Pops is in the driveway, wiping down his blue pickup.

"Hey, Pops!" I call.

He does a double take. Laughs this rumbly, booming laugh that reminds me of Ethan's. "Hello, my girl! And my, don't you look stunning this evening."

He takes my hand and gives me a twirl as a blush rises up my neck. It matters to me what Ethan's grandparents think of me, not only because I'm dating their grandson, but because they've been around for most of my childhood, too. "Thank you. Is Ethan here?"

"He'll be out in a minute, just grabbing a couple odds and ends." Pops smiles, his blue eyes dancing. "You excited for this evening?"

"I guess so... Ethan hasn't told me much about what we're doing."

"I can understand why he wouldn't want to talk about it. Our Ethan does have a hard time keeping secrets from you."

I smirk, leaning in closer. "What kinds of secrets, Pops?"

He booms with laughter. "I'm not going to spoil the fun, my girl! But prepare yourself for what's to come. All good things, of course; Ethan would never want to see you unhappy. He'd do anything for you."

I smile, the heat taking over my cheeks. "I'd do anything for him, too."

"You're here!" The warm voice wraps around me like a blanket, and seconds later, Ethan's strong arms follow.

I turn to loop my hands behind his neck. "I'm here."

He bends to kiss me. "I missed you."

"You saw me, what, three hours ago?"

"Who's counting?" He winks, then steps towards the truck and opens the passenger door for me. "Ready to go?"

I look at Ethan's sweet, smiling face, and then glance at

Pops, who's absolutely beaming next to the truck. All at once, I know that I'm all in. No matter what happens after senior year or the next year or any year after that, I want to and will fight for this relationship. My story with Ethan isn't even just a page in a book, he's the whole freaking book.

My eyes lock on his. "I'm ready."

23

ETHAN

*W*ow.

That is the only word that comes to mind when I see Val coming out of her room. It's not eloquent or original, I know. But I've never had my brain fall out of my head quite like it does when I see her.

And for today, she's all mine.

"Hey, you," I say softly when she approaches, not caring how intimate it sounds.

"Hey, yourself." She tucks her hair behind her ears shyly. It's down for the first time all trip, her curls hanging loosely around her shoulders and framing her face. "You okay? Do I have sunscreen on my mouth again?"

I force myself to look away, to shake my head. But I'm feeling a bit brazen, so I say, "Nope. You just look... beautiful."

She laughs and a flush spreads across her chest and up her neck. I love to see her like this. Her huge eyes are ringed with the slightest amount of makeup, but what draws me in is the sweet, clever sparkle in their depths. "So *cheesy*. You ready for the picnic?"

"Ready when you are. I've got everything in the car."

Last night, sometime between almost kissing her at the water slide, watching her scarf down a burger at Billy's, and dropping her off at her door while not wanting to let her go, I made a decision. Val and I belong together. Val is who I want for my future, the person I want to grow old with and sit on a porch with and build a house for... like that idiot who swung from a ferris wheel in *The Notebook*.

This "last chance road trip," as I've coined it, is my opportunity to show her that I want to be with her. That I'll fight for her, no matter where our lives take us. And today, I'm going to make an extra effort to "court her," as her books call it.

Ugh. Getting sappy again.

Val and I head to the truck and it's all I can do not to take her hand. We drive to the nearby Triple Peak Park, chatting easily the whole time. The park is, conveniently, a spot on Pops's list as well as being a sun-soaked, tree-covered, beautiful patch of land that's perfect for a date. When we were younger, Val loved to feed the ducks and geese that swam in the ponds, and we'd rent those little paddleboats and go for races down the rivers.

Today, I've got all that planned, and more.

Val and I spend the morning walking through the park, following the twisting trails over small hills and through the trees. We talk about nothing and everything, having aimless conversations about favorite TV shows or which 1D member we like best (not my style of music, but a guy's gotta respect Harry Styles).

When the sun gets too hot and our stomachs start growling, Val claims a spot near the lake while I grab the picnic basket. I spread out a blanket for us, and Val crosses her legs in front of her, dipping her head back to soak up the sun.

I watch her for a minute before unpacking the cooler within the basket, laying out hams, cheeses, breads, veggies, and fruits. The icing on the cake (excuse the pun) are the brownies I baked in the hotel kitchen this morning (the owner was kind enough to let me use it).

"I'm so stuffed, I don't think I can eat another bite," Val says as she lolls back on her elbows after enjoying our makeshift charcuterie. "You've done it. You've satisfied the beast."

"You sure about that?" I grab the last container from the cooler. "I can't even tempt you with brownies?"

At this, Val sits straight up. "You brought brownies, too?"

"Of course I did. I wouldn't take you out without bringing brownies. *That* would be lunacy."

She smiles at the container. "I could probably make room for *one* brownie. But only if you promise that we won't walk around anymore and will instead be lazy on this blanket for awhile."

I hand her the container and she pops it open. She does a little shimmy as she picks up one brownie and licks her lips.

All of a sudden, I'm nervous. I watch her reaction carefully.

She frowns as she stares at the treat. "You've never made these for me before. What kind of brownie is it?"

"Guess."

She gives the brownie a hesitant sniff. "Peanut butter? You made me peanut butter brownies?"

"I did."

She stares at the brownie with one brow raised, the picture of skepticism. "You know I—"

"Don't like peanut butter brownies? I know, but I wanted to try baking them, and I thought they tasted pretty good, so I brought these for you."

Val stares at the brownie, back to me, back at the

brownie. I think she might say no.

"Give it a try. If you hate it, you can spit it out and throw me in the lake."

Val's eyes brighten. "I'm holding you to that."

She takes a tiny bite of brownie. Chews slowly. Takes a slightly bigger bite.

She seems pensive, chewing with this adorable frown. I watch her closely as she finishes the square. "Well?" I ask.

"It was... okay."

"Just okay?"

"Just fine." But she reaches for the container again. "I should have one more, just to check—"

"Ah-ha! So you did like it." I laugh, wrenching the container out of her grasp. "Hang on, Teeny. I'm grabbing one, then you can have another."

I take one of the brownies, then innocently place the container on my other side. She shoots me a glare, then moves towards me, reaching across my body. Her pomegranate shampoo fills my nostrils as she almost falls across my lap. I move the container above my head, and she presses her hands on my shoulders as she scrambles to grab it. "Come on, Ethan!" She laughs.

"Wait your turn," I tease her.

She sits back on her heels, pouting, and I take a bite of my brownie.

I barely catch the light in her eyes, the flash of mischief, before...

She bites down on the other side.

Her face is literally inches away, her gaze level and locked with mine. She seems almost as surprised as I am by what she did, but I don't mind it one bit. Having Val's face so close is completely fine with me.

She bites down and sits back, chewing triumphantly. Her hip is pressed against my thigh, and her soft, bare skin is so tempting to run my fingers across. The brownie dries in my mouth and I almost reluctantly chew it.

Let's do that again.

But Val has other ideas. She licks her lips, methodically licks the tops of her fingers from when she grabbed the brownie earlier. "Okay, I'm ready."

"Ready for what?"

"To throw you in the lake."

"What? Why?"

"It's only fair." She shrugs. "I liked the brownie, but I didn't like it *that* much."

"I'm not sure I believe you."

She smiles angelically, but her eyes are full of a challenge. "What? You scared?"

"Absolutely not."

"So do it."

I feel like we're teenagers, having one of those ridiculous banter-y, flirty fights. I consider the lake ahead of us, and maybe I do want to jump in. After all, it *is* really hot, and I could use some cooling down from the whole *Lady and the Tramp* brownie sharing moment.

Without another word, I stand and take my shirt off. Val's eyes grow wide and her gaze lingers on my shoulders and chest for two heated seconds. Then, her eyes drop to my forearm. "That's new," she blurts.

I rotate my arm a little, but I already know what she's talking about. I cock an eyebrow at her. "Never seen a tattoo before, Teeny?"

She shrugs. "Not on you."

I place my other hand over the small tattoo and flex my forearm, remembering every detail of the hours I sat with the tattoo artist. How meaningful it felt. "I got it done right before my grandma died. To remember my childhood and family."

Val nods and I register the way her eyes trace the small, intricate, swooping design, inlaid with an H for Holmes. She probably doesn't see the V hidden in there. Val is as much a part of my history as anyone else.

"It looks nice," she says quietly.

Her eyes rise to meet mine and my heart slams in my chest. Feeling suddenly bold, I reach for her and pick her up. Sling her over my shoulder like I did at the water park.

"What're you—" she screeches. "NOT AGAIN, ETHAN!"

But it's too late because I'm running for the lake with her over my shoulder. I jump in, plunging us both underwater. Val kicks out away from me, and when I come to the surface, she splashes me in the face.

"You are a child!" she yells, laughing. "An absolute child!"

I swim towards her, laughing too, and her hands reach for my shoulders. She pulls herself towards me, and I cradle her hips. It's shallow enough that I can stand, holding her up.

"What can I say?" I smile at her. Her mascara's running and her hair is sopping wet, but this might be my favorite look yet. "You bring out the best in me."

Val bites her lip to hold back a smile. But as I hold her close, neither of us is laughing anymore. The water is cool around us, but all I can feel with startling clarity is every single place where we're touching—her legs around my waist, her forearms resting on my shoulders.

My gaze doesn't break from hers as I lift a hand and press it to her cheek. She's blushing, her cheeks a sweet pink, and I remember the way I traced her lip at the water park. How much I wanted to kiss her then, too. She moves her cheek against my palm and closes her eyes briefly as her lips part.

What happens next is instinct. Muscle memory.

Val's hands tighten behind my neck as I move towards her. Our lips meet, and I know for sure that this isn't a daydream. This kiss is as real as could be. As real as I thought it would never be again.

I pull her against me, and she scrambles up slightly, locking her forearms behind my neck. My hand finds her face so I can deepen the kiss, and she tangles her fingers into my hair. I drink her in, kissing her as I wished I could over the last four years.

I tilt her head back, and break from her lips to kiss down her jawline. Coming back to Val in this moment feels like the world righting itself again.

"Wait," she murmurs. "We should stop."

I stop. Val moves her hands from my hair and lays them flat on my chest. Her eyes are wide and wild and her breath is coming in little gasps.

My grip on her loosens and I step back, away from her. "I'm sorry, Val. I didn't... I thought you—"

"It's okay," Val says quickly. "No, I wanted to. I *want* to. But we haven't spoken in four years and now you're here and..." She trails off. Blinks. "This is a lot to process."

I nod, completely understanding where she's coming from. So many feelings are coming up so fast. "I get that."

"Yeah. I... need some time."

I swallow, happy that I didn't overstep her boundaries but unsure what she means. Regardless, I want her to feel comfortable. "Of course, whatever you need."

"Okay," she says quickly. "Thanks."

With that, she swims back to the shore, and I stand alone for a minute.

Time. I need to give her time to trust me again.

But our road trip ends tomorrow... so time may be the one thing I don't have.

24

ETHAN

Four Years Ago

W hat a waste of time.

   Seriously, what kind of guy plans a whole preposal treasure hunt for the girl he loves only to forget the one, key item the entire evening is centered around?

   I left Val with my grandparents so I could run the ten blocks back to my house. It's a cool evening so I'm not too sweaty, although the memory of Val in that beautiful dress gets my heart racing triple time. I've never considered myself to be one of those guys who loses their minds over a nice sundress (i.e. my friend Noah), but it took me a minute to gather myself. The blue fabric skated along her body, hugging her curves and skimming to her mid-thigh. She looked ethereal. Too good to be real.

   By the time I reach my house, I've undone the top button of my dress shirt and rolled up the sleeves. I suck in a couple inhales to stabilize my breathing before walking inside. Mom's sleeping to prepare for her shift; I haven't seen her over the last couple days, but she has tomorrow off so we'll have dinner and I'll tell her about how things go tonight.

I unlock the door and walk inside. I don't bother kicking off my shoes, just tiptoe down the hall towards the kitchen. It's a little bank robber-y, but I don't want to wake Mom before her alarm.

As I approach the kitchen, I hear a noise. Little snuffles around the corner.

My senses go on high alert and I freeze.

Someone's in the house. Maybe a... raccoon?

Oh, man. The raccoons better not be coming for revenge after Val's little white lie about the carrot patch. I knew sneaking around was a bad idea.

But regardless of this being a gang of raccoons out for blood, or an ordinary house burglar, this whole snuffling thing is not good. I tiptoe back a couple paces and grab the shoe horn. I stand for a moment, psyching myself up to pop out and either scare away the intruder(s) or engage in a shoe horn sword fight. Whatever this comes down to.

Finally, I step out. "What're you—"

I stop in my tracks, shoe horn held aloft.

"Mom?!"

She whips around in her chair at the kitchen table. "Ethan! What're you doing here?" She frowns. "What's with the shoe horn?"

I lower my arm sheepishly. "I thought... Well, I heard noises."

Mom swipes at her cheek. "And you thought the solution was to grab the shoe horn?"

"Yeah? I thought you were sleeping. I figured I'd have to protect you."

"Oh, my boy." Mom chuckles, but the sound is tired. "What would I do without you?"

I frown, now realizing that Mom's nose is red and her

eyes are glassy. Is that mascara streaking down her cheek? "What's wrong?"

"Nothing," she says too quickly. Puts on a bright smile. "Everything's fine. I couldn't sleep."

I pause, take in the way she's avoiding my eyes, the way she brushes at her cheeks again. "Mom, what's going on?"

She holds her breath, seems to consider her options. I keep my gaze patiently, levelly focused on her. Finally, she deflates. "I got some news today. Some *great* news."

Her demeanor does not scream "good news!" It screams "oh hey, life sucks," but I decide not to contradict her. "What kind of great news?"

"I got a job. A really, really good job." Now, the corners of her mouth tip up in a genuine smile. Relief floods her features. "It's Head of Security, and I'll have a *much* more flexible schedule. No more night shifts."

My eyebrows shoot up. "That's amazing!"

"It is. But..." She swallows thickly. "The job's in Montana."

The world comes to an abrupt halt.

"I'm sorry, what?" I ask.

"It's in Aston Falls. Montana." Mom looks miserable again. "I applied months ago, knew it was a long shot that I'd even get an interview. But then, I got the interview, and I figured it was an even *longer* shot that I'd get the job. But here we are..." Her mouth purses. "I'm the new Head of Security at the Aston Falls Medical Center. It's a fantastic opportunity."

"Wow..." I force myself to breathe. In, out, hold it for a second. Try not to freak out. "So, what does this mean?"

"The job starts in a couple weeks. Which means that I only have a short period of time to pack up and move." Mom's frown deepens again. "I... I want to leave it up to you whether you come with me. You're an adult now. Val, your

126

school, your entire life is here. You can make the choice to come with me to Aston Falls, or to stay here with Pops and Nana."

"I'll go with you," I say automatically. Because despite the shock of this revelation, I already know in my gut that I'm not leaving Mom. She needs me as much as I need her.

"Are you sure? You should think about it."

"I don't have to think about it." I shake my head, the movement jerky. "I'm going with you."

My mind is already fifteen steps ahead, considering how on earth I'm going to tell my friends, how my grandparents will feel. And of course... *How am I ever going to leave Val?*

I can't wrap my head around that last part right now, so I clear my throat. "What about Gerry?"

Mom has been dating Gerry for a little over a year. He's a nice guy; he helps out sometimes when things are hectic. Now, she swallows with difficulty. "I just told him. He... ended it. Said he loved me, but he didn't think it was enough to make it work with the distance. He thinks we're better off apart."

Her voice barely conceals a sob, and my heart splits in two. My grandparents and I thought that Mom and Gerry were serious. The fact that he broke things off at this hurdle... well, it's shocking. On top of every other shock of the last two minutes.

"I'm so sorry, Mom," I say, striding over to give her a hug.

"It's okay, I'm okay. Better that I know now than attempt a long distance relationship that was doomed to fail."

My entire body stiffens and I can't bring myself to respond. For some reason, I remember what Pops said earlier today about how lucky Val and I are to be such good friends. He said that our friendship will carry us through anything, but what if I break her heart? What if long distance doesn't work for us either and it breaks her heart?

I've planned for and wanted to do this pre-posal for so long. Wanted to show Val exactly how much she means to me, and how committed I am to her. But how can I make this gesture now, knowing that I'm going to leave and that we haven't talked about it?

Mom sits back, squeezes her eyes shut and opens them again. She attempts a smile. "But what're you doing here? Isn't tonight the big surprise?"

I blink, still caught up in my thoughts. "Yeah... yeah, that's happening tonight. But I can cancel. I can find another night if you want me to stick around."

"Don't be silly! Please, go. I'll be fine. In fact, maybe I'll ask Nana to come over and we can have some tea. You've done more than enough. And tell Val I say hi, in between all of the excitement, of course."

Mom stands to make tea, urging me, once again, to go. I grab the small box on the table next to the kitchen door, still not sure what I should do.

25

VAL

O h, my giddy GOSH!
Ethan kissed me. In a lake. Surrounded by
seaweed and water spiders (probably) and it was the most
romantic, swoony thing I've experienced in a very long time.

So much for putting the past in the past. It's just so easy
to pick up where things left off, like the last four years didn't
happen. Like we've been together and connected this whole
time. The more time I spend with Ethan, the more I realize
that I never truly got over him. That I want him as much
now as I did back then.

It's terrifying, though. Because the last four years *did*
happen. When I was with Randal, I loved him, I really did...
but being with Ethan now is like a part of me being
returned. He has a hold over me and I don't want us to
let go.

So here I am, watching from a helpless distance as my
heart once again throws itself off a cliffside and into Ethan
Holmes bliss.

Buzzz!!!

My phone's vibration on the night stand makes me
jump. I check the screen and bite my lip guiltily when I see

that it's my mom. I promised I'd send her regular updates on the road trip and I haven't sent a single text.

"I'm sorry!" I sing upon picking up.

"Valentina Brynn, there you are!" Mom scolds me lightly. "Your dad and I thought Ethan might've kidnapped you and brought you to Paris or something."

"No Paris," I say, my voice uneven. "Just the good ol' Colorado countryside."

"Glad to hear you're alive, at least. Is this a good time to talk? How's the trip been? Any memorable updates?"

Of course my mom would blow past that first question.

"It's been great!" My voice is so fake-sweet, it makes my teeth hurt. "Ethan and I have been having a great time. So many great activities."

Yeah, say "great" one more time.

"I see." Mom sounds concerned. Rightfully so. "Well, it sure sounds like things are going pretty *great* over there."

"Absolutely. Couldn't be better."

"And have you two talked about anything... special?"

I know what she's hinting at, but I decide to play dumb. I can barely wrap my own head around the fact that Ethan and I made out, let alone tell my mother about it. "Sure, we've talked about music, and TV shows, and bands we like, and—"

"You know what I mean, Valentina. Have you talked about the fact that you used to be *in love*?"

"In love..." I repeat dumbly.

"Yes." Mom's voice is carefully patient. "That boy loved you, and you loved him. I thought this trip might bring up old feelings, maybe light that fire again... No?"

My throat's thick. I can barely swallow.

"No?" I squeak. "Yes? Maybe?"

Back to the mouse impressions. Fantastic.

"How convincing."

I clear my throat. Mom and I are close; it's not surprising that she's seeing right through my denial. I take a deep inhale, hold it in, then say in a rush, "Ethan-and-I-kissed."

"You did!" Mom coos. She doesn't even sound surprised. "When did this happen?"

"Uh... a little while ago when we were at the park. We're back at the hotel now."

"I *knew* this would happen! Your father owes me ten dollars. So what does this mean?"

"Nothing? We haven't talked about it. I stopped it."

"Why?!"

"I don't know, Mom." I sigh. "After everything with Randal, I want to be single for awhile. Be alone. Really sort myself out, you know?"

"Well, that's just plain stupid."

I blink. "What?"

"You know why Dad and I gave you so much free rein when you were younger? Because you *always* knew who you were. You have a good head on your shoulders, mija. You mediated Carmen and Alicia's fights, and acted as a sounding board for your brothers. You are plenty 'sorted out' just as you are. You are perfectly perfect."

A lump is forming in my throat. "Mo—"

"You and Randal broke up six months ago, yes? And I could tell that breakup was coming *for awhile*." She tuts. "I understand that you want to be single, and I'm so supportive of you if that's what your heart wants and needs right now. But I also want you to be sure that you're not running away or ignoring your feelings out of fear."

Her words sting as they hit home. "It just hurt so much when he left... I don't ever want to feel that way again."

"There's no way to guarantee that you'll never get hurt, mija. But you can't live your life on the sidelines, one foot out of everything you do because you're scared. Love and life are messy, and feelings get hurt. You have to find a way to forgive and move on."

"I have forgiven him, Mom. But that doesn't mean I can forget."

"No one is telling you to forget anything. I'm just saying that you have to keep going. Because when the stars align and things go *right*... whew. Love is always worth fighting for. My advice is simply not to run away from someone who's showing you his whole heart."

At that moment, there's a knock at the adjoining door.

"I have to go," I whisper into the phone. "Love you, Mom."

We hang up and I rise to a stand. Take a moment to collect myself before opening the door to Ethan.

He gives me a small, tentative smile. "Can I come in?"

I gesture for him to come through, and he sits on the edge of my bed. It's almost comical how large he seems in here. He takes up all the space, sucks everything towards him like he has his own energy field.

I sit on the other corner of the bed, slightly out of reach of him.

He rubs his jaw, his brows drawn together. "I wanted to say again that I didn't mean for that to happen earlier. Kissing you. I mean, I wanted it to happen, but not like that."

I fiddle with the bedspread. "It's okay."

"No, I get where you were coming from, Val, and I get why you stopped it. It's been a lot these past few days. You need to trust me again. I *want* you to trust me again."

I take a breath, exhale. "This isn't all on you, Ethan. I wanted to kiss you, too."

He glances my way, and his brown eyes are so vulnerable and sweet that my heart somersaults. "Really?"

"Of course." I look away, clear my throat. "It's hard not to feel that way with you."

"I feel the same way. I just... want to do things right with you."

"So why did you do it?"

Ethan waits a beat, and when he speaks, his voice is solid. Certain. "Because I've wanted to kiss you again for a long, long time. Four years' worth of long times."

For some reason, I distinctly remember the last time I asked him this question. This is a better answer. The answer of someone who's thought this through. But even so, I can't bring myself to meet his eyes. Instead, I stare at the bedspread. Why does every roadside hotel have the same loud, splotchy blankets? It seems like such an odd choice to get people to relax...

Focus, Val!

"I don't know where to go from here," I say quietly.

Ethan shifts. "I know. This is... complicated. I'd be lying if I said that spending all this time with you didn't feel right. But I'm happy to pretend the kiss never happened, if that's what you want."

I genuinely can't imagine being able to forget about that kiss. My lips are still tingling with the memory of his mouth, and my body heats at the mere thought of being wrapped around him in the water.

I shrug, risking a glance his way. "That kiss was pretty memorable."

Ethan's lips—pressed into a concerned line—now tug up at the corners. He's shifted to face me. "Oh, yeah?"

My heart is banging around my ribcage so loudly, I'm surprised he can't hear it. "Yeah. I... might be open to another one someday."

His expression shifts and he leans slightly towards me.

That invisible thread between us feels suddenly undeniable.

"I want to be honest with you, Teeny." His voice is low and gruff, like a wave about to break. "I wanted today to feel like a date without actually asking you out, and I realize now that that was stupid. So I want to tell you, point blank, that I want to win you back. I want to date you, court you, whatever you want to call it. I want to be the man for you because I'm still crazy about you. Have never stopped being crazy about you."

His eyes are a storm of contradictions—a mixture of tenderness and fierceness, passion and calm. And yet, through it all, he seems set. Determined.

My stomach is a mess of butterflies and nerves. I focus on the blanket again. "You're serious?"

"Serious as I've ever been."

My mom's words come back to me. *If he's showing you his whole heart...*

All of a sudden, I wonder whether she's right. I've been so consumed with not repeating the past, not moving backwards. But in doing so, have I closed myself off to what's happening right here and now?

New Val would be brave. She wouldn't run away from what she's feeling.

I make a decision. Finally meet his gaze. "Okay... let's give it a shot."

There, I said it. Put it out in the open. And the smile that brightens Ethan's face makes my heart ache. "Prepare yourself, Teeny, you don't know what's coming for you. I'm going to date you so hard."

I laugh. "That sounds ambitious."

"I'm a very ambitious person," he jokes and his expression becomes tender again. "But we'll take it as slow as you feel comfortable with."

His face is full of this innocent joy that makes me want to be closer to him. I scooch over slightly. He places his hands by his side. Not pushing me or urging me to come closer, but there for when I'm ready.

"Whatever makes you happy," he says. "I just want to be with you."

I giggle. "You said that already."

"I'll say it again. However many times you want to hear it."

My legs have somehow developed minds of their own and are now draped over his thighs. His arm cradles behind my back, and he holds me as I rest my head on his shoulder. Everything feels disjointed, but not in a bad way. More like things falling into place after being out of whack for awhile.

"You're such a sap," I murmur.

"Only around you."

I lift my head to look at him. His fingers trace my jawline and his gaze scours my face like he's memorizing my features. His hands are so gentle, his movements so calculated and careful, like he's imagined doing this thousands of times.

His eyes lock on mine again and my breath catches. I would be *very* okay with having a repeat of that kiss right about now.

As though he can read my mind, Ethan bends his head slightly and brushes my lips with his. I tangle my hands in his hair to kiss him properly, but he pulls back.

"Not so fast," he whispers, his voice warm near my ear. "Next time I kiss you, it's not going to be in a random hotel room next to the highway. Next time I kiss you, it's going to be perfect."

26

ETHAN

W ell, we did it.

No, not *that*. We haven't kissed again. Though that is high on my agenda after last night.

We finished the road trip treasure hunt. Pops's final request.

I run my fingers across my scruff as Val and I speed along the highway towards Mirror Valley in Pops's prized blue truck... Now, officially my blue truck. And I'll prize it as much as he did, though less so because it's a "wonderful piece of machinery," and more because it'll always bring back memories with him.

"What're you thinking?" Val asks.

I shoot her a glance, and she actually takes my breath away for a moment. I'm such a *sap*. But I don't mind it so much anymore. "Thinking about Pops."

Val rubs her thumb along the top of my hand. It's a supremely comforting gesture, one that somehow communicates a perfect blend of sympathy and understanding. *It's a thumb, Ethan.* "It must be tough to finish the treasure hunt."

"It is. Tougher than I thought it would be."

We just left our last stop—Paddy's farm. Paddy had a

small petting zoo when we were growing up, and Val and I used to feed the goats and horses, brush them, sweep up straw...

Which, in retrospect, were probably chores that Paddy had to do anyway. Overexcited children let loose near baby goats are cheap labor.

"Did I tell you that my suitcase opened when I was checking out and my stuff spilled everywhere?" Val blurts. "My shampoo and body wash and underpants and pajamas went flying across the lobby. That'll teach me to buy a cheapo bag with a flimsy lock."

I chuckle. I know what Val's doing; I appreciate that she tries to cheer me up when I'm sad. Little does she know that her presence alone makes me happier than anything else could.

"See? Streak of bad luck," I tease her.

"*Don't* call it that." Val shakes her head, but I'm glad to see that she's smiling.

"Bad luck or not, I'm happy you came with me on this trip." I bring her hand to my lips.

"Don't get it wrong." She smiles angelically. "I didn't do this for you."

I give her a look and she giggles, relaxes back into the seat. She makes wave motions out the window, like she did when we first started this trip. It feels like so long ago; so much has changed...

I couldn't be happier for it.

When I went to Val's room last night, I intended only to apologize and assure her that we were on the same page. Instead, she told me that she also wanted to kiss me, and I was over the moon about it. I'm happy to take our time dating and getting to know each other again. As long as I'm with her.

"Do you think Pops did this on purpose?" she asks.

"Like, sticking us together on a road trip. Do you think he knew this might happen?"

"What would happen?" I ask. I want to hear her say it.

Val lolls her head my way. "That you and I would come back together. Date. Whatever."

My smile widens and I give her another look, one that lingers as I get lost in the way the morning sun brings out the yellow flecks in her irises. "I think he knew. Pops rarely did anything without an agenda. I think he was the world's feistiest ninety-one-year-old matchmaker."

"Cheers to that." Val raises her water bottle in a toast. She takes a long drink while I take a swig of my coffee. At that moment, the song on the radio switches and Val leans forward. "I love this one!"

She turns up the volume—without asking this time, I notice—and sings along to a Journey song. I hum, too (on a quieter level), feeling totally at peace. For the first time, I'm seeing my future and I can't wait for for it to start.

Who knew that a single weekend, a single road trip could change literally everything?

"Ooh, a gas station!" Val points at the dilapidated building with the same level of excitement that she had at the water park. "Can we stop? I have to pee."

I signal to turn off the highway. "You and your pee breaks."

"What? It's not my fault I have the bladder of a pregnant lady."

Val says this lightly, but all at once, my mind is filled with visions of a pregnant Val. How wonderful of a mother she'd be, how amazing it would be to start a family with her. To raise kids with her in a big house with an even bigger backyard.

Slow down, Ethan. One step at a time.

As soon as I stop the car, Val runs for the gas station. I

make to follow her, but as I grab my phone, I see an email notification.

It's Carolyn at the Aston Falls Express. They want my answer by end of day tomorrow.

So much for taking the weekend off.

But the conversation with Val has stayed with me. She knows me better than anyone, even after four years apart. She managed to put words to a dream I wasn't even aware I had, a dream I never *let* myself have. But the more I've thought about it, the more right it feels.

I want to have a bakery. To spend my days making delicious treats and baked goods for entire families to enjoy together. Like I did with my family.

So last night, after working things out with Val, I did some research and talked to my mom at length. Now, I'm certain about what I want and where I'm going next.

I open a reply and start typing.

Hi Carolyn. I've put a lot of thought into your offer. I want to thank you for the opportunity, and...

My fingers fly across the screen as I commit to the easiest decision I've ever made. I click "send" and with a deep exhale, I relax against the seat.

Four years ago, I made a decision to walk away from the woman I love.

I won't ever make that mistake again.

27

VAL

Four Years Ago

"Sorry I'm late, Teeny."

Ethan's jogging up the driveway. He runs a hand through his hair and shakes it out a little. I smile, my heart fluttering again. Man, he looks so good in the twilight. Even better than Rob and Taylor in *Twilight*. I am Team Ethan all the way.

He stands next to Pops, who slaps his shoulder. "You found what you were looking for, son? Hope you didn't wake your mom."

A shadow passes over Ethan's face, but the next second, it's gone. "She was already awake. She... couldn't sleep."

"Those nights are the worst." I scrunch up my nose. "Especially when it's too hot and there's no AC. It's violent."

"Been there," Ethan says with a secret twinkle. His expression goes serious again as he looks back at Pops. "Is Nana around? She should call Mom."

"Nana's inside checking on dinner. I'll let her know to call

140

your mom." Pops points at the truck. "Now, you kids are already getting a late start. Best get on the road, don't you think? Can't have you crashing my princess because it's too dark."

Ethan's face relaxes in a laugh and I chuckle, too. His eyes meet mine, and there's not even a hint of the concern I thought I saw in him. I must've imagined it. Or maybe he's nervous for what's to come. With all the to-do around this evening—all of the mysterious comments Pops was making during our conversation and the secret smiles at the truck— I'm starting to feel a little nervous myself.

"Let's go, Teeny," Ethan says, taking my hand.

We pile into Pops's pickup and Ethan starts the engine. We get moving without a hitch.

I turn to him eagerly. "*Now* can you tell me what we're doing?"

Ethan laughs, shifts into third gear as we drive out of the neighborhood. "Alright, you've been patient. We're doing a treasure hunt."

My heart leaps with excitement. "Really?!"

"Well, *you* are doing a treasure hunt. I'm acting as chauffeur for the night." He gives me a wink.

"What's my first clue?"

For the next couple of hours, Ethan and I drive to different stops in Mirror Valley. First is the Valley Roast, where I find a regency romance novel hidden in an alcove next to the door. That leads us to my favorite bookstore, open late so that I could find a container with a brownie behind my go-to reading chair.

After that, it's off to the school field where Ethan and I had our first kiss. There, I find a letter with a sweet message. Next is the treehouse, and Ethan and I climb inside to find that the place has been refurnished. New blankets and pillows are spread throughout, and taped glow-in-the-dark stars blink on the ceiling. "Because this is our place, just you and me," he explains.

That brings us to our final destination: his grandparents' house. At this point, I'm already reeling with emotion and nostalgia. I can't believe Ethan did this; set up this entire evening for me. Every stop—and every gift along the way—was so meaningful. I haven't even eaten the brownie yet because I don't think I can swallow around the lump in my throat.

On his part, Ethan's been uncharacteristically quiet and thoughtful all evening. I've asked him if something's on his mind, but every time I do, his brow clears and he comes back to me. I've chalked it up to nerves about the treasure hunt—he'll be back to normal as soon as we're done.

Ethan parks the truck in the driveway and we sit for a moment. The glow of the porchlights gives him this dreamy, romantic aura. Like a warm filter has descended on the world.

"You ready for the last step?" he asks, his voice low.

I breathe in, suddenly weirdly nervous. I have a feeling that what comes next is going to be the pinnacle of the evening. This has to be why he's been so quiet. "I think so."

Ethan opens his door, but before he can leave, I grab his arm and pull him back towards me. I tangle my fingers in his hair and my lips find his. "Thank you for doing this," I whisper. "But why tonight?"

A half-smile plays on his lips. "You'll see."

He hops out of the truck and opens the door for me. We walk around the house to the backyard.

My jaw drops.

Twinkling fairy lights are strung across the yard, interspersed with shining, colorful orbs. The patio table is covered with candles, and my preferred chair—the cozy white loveseat—has been moved into the grass facing the moon. It's beautiful; completely transformed from where Ethan and I were laying hours ago.

My heart is racing. "What's going on?"

"This is the end of the treasure hunt."

"It's incredible."

"Like a scene out of *Pride and Prejudice*?"

"Better than any movie."

"I thought..." Ethan trails off into silence.

"Thought what?" I prompt. When I look up at him, he's staring through the kitchen window into the house. I follow his gaze to where his Nana is giving his mom a hug. Their faces are turned away from the light.

Ethan's quiet for so long, his demeanor suddenly rigid and tense. I scan his face. "Ethan?"

No answer. There's an expression on his face I don't recognize, but that makes my stomach clench uncomfortably. He taps his pants pocket absentmindedly.

"Ethan," I say again, louder this time. "Is everything okay?"

He barely flinches. Finally, he takes a breath—a hesitant breath, if I'm not mistaken. When he looks at me again, there's a darkness in his eyes that I've never seen before. He gives his head a shake, looks down.

The hairs on the back of my neck stand. "What's going on?"

He's stopped fiddling with his pocket and instead stands straight. "You know you mean the world to me, right?" he says quietly.

I blink. "You mean the world to me, too."

"Well, I don't want to lose you, Teeny."

"What?" My brow puckers in a frown. "Why would you lose me?"

"Mom got some news today." He breathes in, breathes out. "We're moving."

"Like across town?"

"No. To Aston Falls. In Montana."

My heart stops. My arms go limp by my side.

"She got a really good job offer, one she can't turn down." He clenches his jaw. "I have to go with her. You understand that, right?"

"Of course I do," I say quickly. And I mean it, Ethan and his mom are close, they need each other. I'd never expect her to move without him. "So what does this mean?"

Ethan shifts. "I don't want us to be doomed to fail..."

"What are you talking about?"

A pause. Another shift. When Ethan speaks again, his voice is heavy. "I think we should go back to being friends."

My breath catches, a sharp inhale. "Why would we do that?"

"I don't want to hurt you, Val. I can't lose you. So I think the best decision for us is to take a step back. Go back to how things were."

A million arguments rush forward on my tongue, fighting to be released, but the expression on Ethan's face is enough to stop them all. I've never seen him like this. His face is grim but resolute. "So you've decided," I whisper.

"I want to do what's best for you."

I have a hard time swallowing, a hard time breathing. I'm filled with so much raw emotion, my heart hurts. "What was all this about, then?" I ask, gesturing around the yard. "Your way of letting me down easy?"

Ethan's face cracks, and for a moment, he looks so heartbroken. His Adam's apple bobs as he swallows. "It wasn't like that."

I think I'm nodding. I have no idea how I'm still standing given that my legs are numb. The world is crashing around me, and I don't know what to feel, or how to act. I have whiplash from the entire evening—the sweet, meaningful treasure hunt that felt to be leading somewhere that I really, really didn't expect would be here.

"So this is it?" I ask, my voice robotic.

He nods, his face pinched and pale.

I open my mouth, but no words come out. I feel powerless. Nothing I can say, nothing I can do will change what Ethan wants. He's made his decision. When one person stops fighting in a relationship, there's no going forward from there. And Ethan's telling me that he's stopped fighting.

I clear my throat, wrench my mouth shut. After a moment, I force myself to say, "Okay. If that's what you want."

"Val, do me a favor and review today's check-ins to make sure we're ready?"

Ivy's voice interrupts my thoughts as she blows into reception like a whirlwind. She skitters next to me behind the front desk, slightly out of breath.

"Sure thing," I say brightly, as though I haven't spent the past ten minutes staring blankly at the reservation book while actually thinking about Ethan. "We've got the first guests scheduled to come in at 2pm. I've got the keys and welcome packets ready to go, and I added a kids' coloring book as the guest mentioned that their kids love to draw. Easy-erase markers this time, so we don't have a repeat of what happened in Room 3."

Ivy shudders, probably recalling the multi-colored drawings of dinosaurs, flying saucers, and a collection of (hopefully imaginary) creatures splattered across the walls. They weren't even bad drawings—the kid could have a future in art. But stick-figure depictions of smiling giraffe-fish are not what you want in a cozy mountain inn.

"You're a lifesaver." Ivy shakes her head. "Today's been crazy. The lady in Room 5 put birdseed on her window sill to—and I quote—'bring nature to her' and now... well, let's just say that there's a little *too much* nature happening. Specifically involving hungry chipmunks."

My eyes widen. "Eek."

"Eek is right. I haven't had a chance to take a breath this morning, let alone get on top of everything." She clasps her hands, anxious.

I place a hand on her arm, smile reassuringly. "That's what I'm here for."

She nods at me gratefully. At that moment, the front door opens and a guy wearing what looks like a Ghostbuster costume strolls into reception.

"You!" Ivy calls, pointing at the Ghostbuster. "So glad you're here. We are in *desperate* need of a power vacuum. And thanks for driving in from Summer Lakes; our usual housekeeping company said this is above their pay grade, which I do understand, but it's rather inconvenient, as you can imagine. If you'll follow me..."

Ivy stalks off with the guy in tow, leaving me to return to my work.

Not my thoughts about Ethan. Nope.

When we got back from the road trip late last night, Ethan dropped me off. Miraculously, my mom and dad must not have heard the truck as I managed to make it into the house before they could come outside. It's not that I don't want them to see Ethan or know what's going on with us (my mom would be our biggest cheerleader, pompoms and all). The problem is that I'm having a hard time not reliving the last time we finished a treasure hunt together...

Specifically, when he decided to break things off and move to Montana.

It was a complicated situation, I know. I could never fault Ethan for moving with his mom. But what hurt the most was the way he gave up on us. Now, he has this wonderful opportunity back in Montana, and I couldn't be happier for him. But it's hard not to wonder if history's going to repeat itself.

My mind wants to say it won't. Ethan told me that he wants to be with me, but my heart is having a hard time forgetting its scars.

The French doors open and Ivy walks back into reception. Scratch that, she's *skipping* into reception. And talking to a man I don't recognize. He's tall and lanky and has what I can only describe as a baby face.

"HAHAHAHA, Cam, you crack me up," Ivy's saying, her voice tinkling and light.

Cam frowns. "I don't get it."

"What you said about the power vacuum guy looking like an action movie character? I was thinking Ghostbusters? No?"

Crickets.

"Uh, anyway," Ivy says quickly, her cheeks reddening. "What can I do for you today?"

"Are your grandparents here? I'd like to talk to them about my business and what we can do for them." Cam smiles this white, flashy smile, nods back towards the French doors. "Seems I came at the perfect time."

"Oh, yeah. You have a cleaning company, right? Clean Reflections?"

"It's *Clear* Reflections, actually. Don't worry, it's an easy mistake to make."

Ivy's smile tightens slightly. "Right. Well, they should be back later so I'll tell them to call you."

"Perfect. I'll leave my business card so they won't forget."

Cam rifles in the pocket of his fancy blazer for a moment, then produces a stack of white cards. He takes a couple and hands them to Ivy. "In case one gets lost," he adds as an explanation for the second card, but his gaze lingers. "Or, you know, in case you'd like one."

That seems to perk Ivy up a little. "Awesome."

What happens next rivals any streak of bad luck I could ever have...

Ivy shoots out a hand to collect the two cards, but instead, her fingers collide with the stack. The cards go flying, a veritable shower of white confetti flying through the air and scattering across the desk and the floor of the lobby.

"Oh, no!" Ivy squeaks, bustling around to collect the cards. "I'm so sorry!"

"It's fine, it's fine," Cam says, but his tone is short. He scrambles around with her. "Totally understandable."

"That's one way to do a quick delivery," I chime in. Immediately regret how stupid that sounded.

Cam looks at me, raises a brow. "And you are?"

"Val. The new receptionist."

"The *awesome* new receptionist," Ivy adds with a wink. I smile, appreciating that she's in my corner.

"Anyway, have your grandparents call me." Cam flashes Ivy another smile. "I hope to see you again soon. Real soon."

"Great." Ivy full on blushes now.

Oh yeah, she *definitely* likes this guy.

As soon as Cam leaves, I turn on her. "Okay, your turn to spill. What is up with you and baby face man?"

Ivy purses her lips. "He doesn't have a baby face. He's just... cute."

"He has dimples for *days*."

Ivy laughs. "Nothing's happened with him, but maybe I kind of want it to. Problem is, whenever he's around, I have zero coordination. You saw what happened with his business cards, it's like that all the time. Don't even think about giving me a cup of coffee around him..." Her expression turns dreamy. "Mmh. Speaking of, I would love some coffee right about now."

"Same. I only had one cup this morning." That's probably why I keep getting distracted. Yes, coffee will fix my distraction situation, and then I can get my head back into work. Easy peasy. "I'll do a coffee run."

"You're a lifesaver on all counts today, Val. I promise I'll add 'find a coffee supplier' to my to-do list."

I chuckle as I grab my purse. And maybe because I've been so caught up in my thoughts of Ethan all morning, when he walks in the front door of the Brookrose, it takes me a minute to process that he's actually *here*.

His deep brown eyes land on me and he smiles this yummy, heart-stopping smile that makes my legs weak.

"Just the girl I'm looking for," he says as he approaches the front desk.

"Hey, Ethan," I say, feeling almost shy. I clear my throat, remind myself that I'm at work. "I'm about to run out for coffee."

"Great. There's something I want to talk to you about. Can I come?"

Ivy, who now has her nose buried in the reservation book, waves a hand at us. "More hands means more coffee. Now that the chipmunk situation is sorted, I'll get on top of everything here."

Ethan's eyebrows pop up. "Chipmunk situation?"

I shake my head. "I'll tell you as we walk. Coffee first, then chipmunks."

There's a sentence I never thought I'd say.

29

VAL

"Wow... What else happened while you were gone on the weekend?" Ethan laughs as we walk down Main Street. At some point while telling him the chipmunk story, he interlaced his fingers with mine, and I'd be lying if I said it didn't feel so completely right to walk hand-in-hand like this.

"That was the top news story." I giggle. "I have a feeling that it's never going to be a dull moment at the Brookrose. I love it already."

"They're lucky to have you."

"I'm lucky to have them. I'm so glad that I found a job there."

"Yeah, Mirror Valley is your home. You love it here."

I nod, a smile on my lips. "Exactly. I couldn't imagine leaving..."

I cut myself off and a weird, loaded silence follows my statement. My heart squeezes and I look up at Ethan, but his face is blank. Is he thinking about the same thing I am—AKA his job opportunity in Montana? What's going to happen with us if he accepts the position?

I can't help but wonder again if we really *can* make this

work. Or whether we only work exclusively in a grandparent's-will-request kind of situation.

Finally, I can't take it anymore. I have to ask.

"Are you—" I start as Ethan says, "I was thinking—"

We both stop, share a glance.

I gesture towards him. "You go first."

"Okay." He rubs his jaw. "I wanted to ask how you're feeling about us."

My heart slams. The man can read my mind, so does he know how nervous I feel about this conversation? "How are *you* feeling about it all?"

Ethan waits a beat, smiles this sweet, tender smile I suspect is reserved only for me. "I'm feeling good, Teeny. Really good."

"Really?" I ask. "You're not having, like, second thoughts or doubts or anything?"

"The only doubt I have is whether I can hold off on kissing you," he teases, and leans down to kiss my cheek, right next to my mouth.

My body breaks out in shivers, but I hold back. Place a palm on his chest. "Are you sure?"

A little crinkle forms between his brows. "Of course. What's on your mind?"

"Nothing," I say quickly. "I just wanted to check."

"When it comes to you, I have no doubts. Are you having doubts?"

"Well..." I trail off. "I can't help but wonder if everything's going to change."

"What do you mean?"

I swallow thickly. Part of me wants to forget this conversation, squash it down, but I have to be brave. I have to be New Val. "You might change your mind."

Now, Ethan comes to an abrupt halt. His hand is loose around mine, but he doesn't let go. "You think I could?"

"You did once before."

Ethan looks visibly shocked. He takes both my hands, looks into my eyes. "I never changed my mind about you, Val. That was never what it was about. Four years ago, I did what I did because I didn't want to lose you. Though, I guess I did anyway..."

I open my mouth, but can't find words to say. We really did lose each other, and I know I'm at least partly to blame for that.

I remember the pain of those few months after he ended it. How I threw myself into dating Randal and how I fought tooth and nail for that relationship, even when it turned out to be the wrong one. I pushed those feelings away for so many years, refused to acknowledge how awful it felt to lose Ethan. He tried to reach out a couple times after moving to Aston Falls, but I never responded. It hurt way too much, and I couldn't deal with it at the time.

"I was heartbroken," I say quietly.

A flash of pain crosses his features. "I can't tell you how many times I've replayed it in my mind. Kicked myself for the way that night went. That was the last thing I wanted to happen."

"So what did you want?"

He gestures towards a bench. We take a seat, and I lift one of my legs under me. "That night, I had a plan for us. My granddad and grandma were involved, even Ray. I put together that treasure hunt, and at the end, there was the biggest surprise of all." His shoulders drop and he looks suddenly defeated. "I had a ring. I wanted to do a pre-posal. Not a *pro*posal because we were so young, but, like, a promise for a proposal."

What?!

He mistakes the reason for my silence. "I'm sure that sounds stupid."

"It doesn't," I manage, my voice mechanic. "You were going to pre-pose to me?"

"I was." Ethan shoots me a glance. "Thing is, I found out just before that Mom and I were moving to Aston Falls, and the thought of losing you—losing what we had, losing our friendship—scared me so much. I didn't want to do wrong by you, do this whole pre-posal thing and then move away. It didn't seem fair to you."

I'm trying to wrap my head around this news. "So you told me that you wanted to go back to being friends..."

"Exactly. I was shocked and caught off guard with the news. And then I spiraled, got so terrified of us having some awful breakup that would destroy our friendship. In the end, it basically happened anyway." Ethan shakes his head, and when he speaks again, his voice is full of emotion. "I can't believe you thought that I changed my mind about you. All I've ever wanted is to be in your life, and to have you in mine."

"Well." I chuckle dryly, still reeling. "We did a good job of that, didn't we?"

Ethan smiles humorlessly, runs his fingers through his hair. His eyes meet mine, and they're so deep and dark and earnest that it takes my breath away. "You never have to worry about me not wanting you. *I* am the one who needs to deserve you, Val, who has to be worthy of a second chance. And I want you to know that I'm going to fight for you. Since spending time with you, it's like my life has righted itself again. *You* are my direction."

His words wash over me—calm, warm, comforting. The walls around my heart continue to crack and crumble as Ethan brings to light the wounds from so long ago, the pain I'd brought with me into the present. I want to believe him. Really, I do.

His eyes search my face. "What're you thinking?"

"I'm thinking…" I take a breath. Then I scramble close to him, nuzzle into his chest. "I had no idea about any of this. Thank you for telling me. And I want you to know that you make me happy, Ethan."

He wraps his arms tight around me, and I sink into his arms.

Then, I take his hand and pull him to a stand so we can keep walking towards the Valley Roast, my heart full and happy.

As soon as we turn the corner towards the cafe, we come to a stop.

"What the…?" Ethan says.

There's a line out the door and a huge crowd milling in front of the cafe.

"What's going on?" I drop Ethan's hand to walk through the crowd. There's a large white banner across the front window. "The Valley Roast's closing?"

"Only a couple months to go," a sing-song voice announces. Fran, our town's eccentric seventy-year-old grandmother is standing behind my left shoulder. She's wearing her favorite pink cowboy hat today. "A long time coming, too. Alan and Darla are gettin' up there."

"That's too bad." I frown. "The Roast's been here for… well, ages. None of their kids wanted to take it off their hands?"

"You know the Brighton kids, they're all off gallivanting across the world." Fran tuts away. "But I wouldn't worry about it. Alan and Darla are ready to let it go, retire, spend time in their garden. Another business will move in soon enough."

I nod. The townspeople in Mirror Valley are pretty scrappy. I'm sure this'll be a new hair salon or dance studio or dry cleaners in no time.

"Anywho. Ethan, dear, I have to congratulate you. Ray

told me about this exciting opportunity in Aston Falls. A fine dining restaurant on a *train* to boot! How totally unique."

"Oh, yeah." Ethan shoots me a glance. "I was pretty honored to be offered such a competitive position."

"So, are you taking it?" Fran asks.

Ethan meets my gaze and my heart jumps.

"No." His eyes are still on me. "I turned it down."

He did *what*?

All at once, my stomach clenches into a painful ball. Ethan's gaze doesn't waver and it occurs to me that he might want me to be happy about this. Happy that he turned down this wonderful job.

Instead, all I feel is an ache deep in my heart. And a desperate need to get out of here.

"Excuse me," I mutter. "I have to go."

"Go?" Ethan frowns. "We don't have the coffees yet."

"It's fine. I'll get them somewhere else." He doesn't drop my hand, so I level him a look that he'll remember he shouldn't mess with. "Let me go, Ethan."

He blinks, drops my hand, and I jog away through the crowd.

30

ETHAN

E**than**: What happened? Is everything okay?

I scrub my fingers across my jaw as I open the text thread one more time. Still no response from Val.

I don't understand what happened at the Valley Roast. One minute, we were talking about chipmunks and I was basically declaring my love for her. The next, she was running away from me through the crowd.

She told me to let her go, so I did. I sent her this text hours ago, but there's been nothing.

I have to assume that it has to do with what I told Fran—that I was turning down the job in Montana. That was the reason I went to see Val today—so I could tell her all of my news.

But why would that make her so upset? I wish I knew what she was thinking so we could talk about it and work through it together. How can we do that if she shuts me out?

I can't help but feel worried. I told Val that I wanted to fight for her, that I wanted to deserve a second chance. But how can I if she refuses to talk to me when she's upset? We finally got to a place where I thought we were moving forward together. Now, she's running away.

I shake my head, put my phone down again. I've been packing and unpacking parts of the house, straightening things up. Now that the road trip has come to an end, it's time to officially say goodbye to Pops, but also to move forward. Aside from the truck, he left me a few things in his will, and I've been saving the things he left Mom for when she visits next.

It would all be a lot easier if a certain wild-haired lawn-mower wasn't constantly on my mind.

A little while later, my phone dings and I jog through the house to grab it.

Val: Meet me at the treehouse.

31

VAL

I shift on my feet, bouncing back and forth in the overgrown grass. My stomach is a ball of nerves and anxiety.

About whether Ethan will come, yes. But also because it's officially nighttime and I can imagine the lurking spiders that are coming out to play. In the past, I only ever came to the treehouse at night when Ethan was with me.

I just hope that he'll be here tonight as well.

I feel terrible for running away earlier. After hearing that he turned down the job in Montana, I couldn't stop thinking that we were heading down the exact same road all over again. Then, I came to a realization: this whole time, I've been worried that Ethan is going to give up on us again...

But what if I've been worrying about the wrong thing all along?

"Teeny?"

The voice fills me with relief. Because A) my spider chaser is here, and B)—most important of all—he *came*.

"I'm over here," I say, then clear my throat. "I'd turn on the fairy lights but..."

"Spiders?"

I chuckle. Shake my head, though he can't see.

In the darkness, the patch of shadow that is Ethan comes to stand right in front of me. Seconds later, we're bathed in the warm glow from the fairy lights in the treehouse. His face is illuminated, detailing every angle of his cheekbones, his strong nose. I spot the auburn hair in his scruff, and the freckles across his cheeks.

Ethan's eyes drop down my body and he smirks as he clocks the tie-dye hoodie I threw on over the skirt I wore to work today. The road trip changed me in more ways than one—including the fact that I don't feel this relentless, stifling pressure to be so sternly clean-cut and prim. "Adult," I used to call it. But Ethan's shown me that I can be easier on myself. That I can be myself.

Which brings me to the crumpled papers I have in my hand.

"I'm glad you texted," he says, his voice low.

"I'm sorry." I shake my head. "I was awful. You told me all of those wonderful things earlier, and then I ran away. I didn't give you a chance to talk, or to say my part. I actually..." I hold up the papers. "I wrote you a letter. I was going to put it in the letter box, but..."

"Spiders." Ethan says this again more definitively, with a teasing, knowing smile.

I nod once. Purse my lips. "See? You know me so well, Ethan. Too well, I think."

"Too well?"

"Yeah. You turned down that job, an amazing job." I pause. "And you knew that I wanted to stay in Mirror Valley."

"I did. On both counts." He frowns. "But I can't understand why you left like that."

I shift again. Remember what Mom said about living

life on the sidelines. I can't have one foot out the door anymore, not when it comes to Ethan. I exhale. "Because hearing that you turned down the job made me wonder if you're giving up on us again."

Ethan blinks. "What?"

"You turning down the job triggered something for me. I worried that you didn't think we could make it if you *did* accept it. That we still couldn't do the distance or something. It brought me back to all those years ago. And that's when I realized something really important..." I fiddle with the papers in my hand. "When we broke up last time, I stopped fighting, too."

Ethan looks like he wants to say something. I keep going, knowing that I need to say this, and he needs to hear it.

"I was thinking of why we fell apart. Back then, I thought I was ready to fight, but I didn't know what that meant. We never talked about it, and I didn't say anything when you ended things. I should've tried instead of cutting you out. But we're not going to repeat history. You said you want to fight for us, and I want to be brave and fight for us, too. And that means putting the past in the past, forgiving, and moving forward. It means talking about the hard stuff, and going all in, as terrifying as that may be."

I pause. Ethan waits. I can't remember the last time I was this honest with anyone, even myself.

"It also means that you can't give up on your dreams in exchange for me." My voice doesn't waver. "You have to do what's best for you, Ethan. I can't stand the idea of you sacrificing your opportunities and giving up what you've worked so hard for. That's not how relationships work —*good* relationships, anyway."

Now, he opens his mouth. "But Va—"

"So we'll figure it out. I *want* to figure it out with you."

My eyes sting a little as I push forward. "You've already given me so much, inspired me in ways you can't understand. I've been trying to be this New Val for so long, this 'highest self' that felt at times completely unattainable. But over the last few days, with you, it was like she and I were one and the same. You help me feel like my best self. You help me feel brave."

There, I said it. All of it.

My heart is out in the open, once and for all. I'm vulnerable and totally exposed.

And Ethan's here with me. Placing a big, warm hand on my cheek. Looking at me with such intensity, my breath catches. "Can I be honest with you now?"

I nod.

"Val, you're my favorite person in the world," he starts. "I would be honored to do long distance with you. But I'm not giving up my dreams by turning down this job, I'm moving towards them."

I frown. "What?"

"You were right," he says. "You were right from the start. I never acknowledged to myself that being a chef wasn't what I wanted until *you* vocalized it. You know me better than I know myself, and the moment you mentioned the bakery thing, the blinds lifted from my eyes."

"So... what do you want then?"

Ethan's lips tug up in a smile. "That's what I was going to talk to you about earlier. I *want* to move back here. I've been chatting with Darla and Alan at the Valley Roast about buying the space. I want to open a cafe like the one that I loved in Aston Falls."

"The Morning one?" I ask faintly.

"Morning Bell, yeah." Ethan's brow darkens. "I'm sorry I didn't talk to you about this earlier. I figured you'd understand seeing as you suggested the whole baking thing originally. Of course I want to do this with you. Make these decisions with you. Whether that's here in Mirror Valley, or in Montana, or somewhere else entirely. I already know that I've got what I need to be happy. And I want to give you the world, because the world is what you deserve."

I shake my head, hardly believing any of this. "You're already giving me the world," I whisper.

His eyes dance. "Not quite."

He reaches into his pocket and presses something cool into my hand. "I've held onto this, could never let it go. It doesn't have to mean anything, but it belongs to you, Val. It always has."

When he pulls his hand away, I see a small, silver ring.

"We're taking it slow, and I'm happy with that," he says quietly. "So take this as my intention to date you and move forward with you. To fight for you even when things get hard, and there are hurdles and obstacles that seem insurmountable. As long as you want that, too."

"I really do, Ethan." I breathe. "I want to fight for you, and I'm ready to."

He places his hands on my cheeks, presses his forehead to mine. "I'm so happy to hear that."

I collapse into his chest and he holds me close. He skims his fingers along my upper arm, sending shivers across my skin.

I tilt my chin to look at him, and his gaze meets mine. In his eyes, I don't see our future or our past. I see our present —two flawed, imperfect individuals who are dedicated to each other. Who believe in something bigger than ourselves, bigger than our mistakes and where tomorrow might take us.

Ethan places kisses across my cheeks, on my nose. Showers my neck with them. I close my eyes and savor the moment.

And when his lips finally, finally, meet mine, I see that he was right. Because everything about this moment is perfect. Everything about this kiss is perfect.

Now, I understand—love is always worth fighting for. And it all started with a road trip.

○ ○

Thank you so much for reading!

If you enjoyed this book, please leave me a review. As a new author, reviews mean everything to me. I appreciate each and every one of them.

WANT MORE LOVE IN MIRROR VALLEY?

Ivy Brooks has hated her brother's best friend since school. When he comes back to Mirror Valley for her brother's wedding, the two are forced to put their differences aside and work together.

Falling for the enemy was never on Ivy's agenda. But nothing goes according to plan when James Weston is around...

Turn the page to start reading The Next Worst Thing.

THE NEXT WORST THING: CHAPTER ONE

IVY

People say that you know when something feels right.

Me? I pay attention when things feel *wrong*. Dead wrong.

Like, when you meal prep a tuna casserole for a crazy week at work, but you're too busy to eat it until four days later. And by then, the pasta's soggy, the tuna smells weird, and you're actually craving pizza. Or when your grandparents take a step back from running your family's cozy mountain inn, and they make you the new manager... but somehow, you still feel like an imposter. Even though you've been prepping for this for years.

Or when your brother's "all about free spirit" fiancée suddenly decides that she wants burnt orange tiger lilies for their wedding. Tiger lilies are gorgeous, but there's no denying that they'll clash horribly with the rest of the pastel blue decor.

Burnt orange and pastel blue. Talk about opposing sides of an issue.

"Are you absolutely *sure* that's what you want?" I ask again, my voice cracking slightly on the end of my sentence.

"How many times do I have to say it?" Eleanor responds in a clipped sigh—very unlike her usual calm, monotonous tone—as she throws her wavy brown hair over her shoulder.

"Of course. Sorry." I make a note on my handy wedding planning clipboard. *Find a way to incorporate bright orange into the color scheme...?* This is Eleanor's wedding, and no matter the clashing colors, I'll defer to her and make it work.

In the past couple weeks, I've gone from "venue coordinator" to "low-budget wedding planner." Make that "free wedding planner." Not that I mind much. Aside from wanting to give my brother and his bride the perfect big day, I do have other, slightly selfish, reasons to be doing this.

At this point, it's actually a little surprising that Eleanor's come forth with an opinion at all—she's spent most of our wedding meetings alternating between tap-tapping on her phone and looking unbelievably bored.

"It's moments like this that tell me how much we *need* to get out of this town," Eleanor goes on, checking her sparkling mauve nails.

I swallow, ignoring the jab. And the subsequent sadness at the thought of my big brother, Luke, leaving town. Eleanor's made it no secret that she intends to move them to San Francisco right after the wedding.

I've spent a lot of time wondering whether things might be different if Eleanor and I got along. Would she—and, therefore, Luke—want to stay in Mirror Valley if we were best friends? For some reason, Eleanor and I never jived, and it bothers me given that Luke is pretty much my favorite human on earth (not that I'd tell him that).

I *should* be able to be friends with his fiancée... right?

"Babe, I know it's been a long day, but there's no need to take it out on Ivy," Luke scolds Eleanor gently.

He rarely says her name these days. Luke's been dating Eleanor Wilkes since high school, but since starting her influencer career as "basically a spiritual healer" three years ago, she insists that we call her "Lenore."

Luke loves Eleanor/Lenore to the ends of the earth, and he'd do anything for her, even stop calling her by her given name. And letting her fill his gorgeous ranch house with the TikTok must-haves she promotes. High-waisted "lifting" yoga pants, sets of crystals in a literal rainbow of colors, and enough incense sticks to build a second home (though, if an accident happened and it burned down, Mirror Valley would smell like patchouli for years to come).

I, however, do not love Eleanor/Lenore to that extent. And so, I tend to mentally refer to her as "Elly," a name which she's made clear she appreciates even less.

And yes, it's kind of petty, and I promise I'm not usually like this. But given the woman's passive-aggressive comments and barely-veiled disdain over the past years, it's the only acceptable way that I can retaliate: in private, without her knowing.

"We'll find some tiger lilies for you," I say pleasantly as I add a note to speak with the florist. "Clarissa should be able to order some."

"Thank you, Ivy. Tiger lilies bring good luck. So if you can't find them and our marriage goes down the drain, we'll know who to blame."

She smiles thinly at her own joke and I cough up a half-hearted laugh.

"Didn't you want to show us the gazebo next?" Luke cuts in tiredly.

"That's right." I shoot them both a beaming smile, and Luke's hazel eyes slice through my saccharine gaze. *Take it easy,* I can almost hear him grumble. I whip around and walk towards the French doors at the far end of the lobby. "Follow me."

My heels click-clack on the hardwood floor. It's a bit ridiculous that I'm showing them around the Inn seeing as Luke and I essentially grew up here.

The Brookrose Inn has been with our family for generations—ever since the founding of Mirror Valley, according to our town's folklore. In fact, it was recently named one of Mirror Valley's heritage sites—an honor that I'm getting printed on all of the Inn's brochures and paperwork. History buffs love stuff like that, and our inn loves history buffs.

Or any buffs, really. Bring on all the buffs.

My grandparents inherited the Inn, and have loved running it for the past forty-plus years. But they're ready to retire and I can't say I blame them. Running an inn is very rewarding, but it's hard work. Or so I've heard, seen, and learned.

I finished my degree in Hospitality Management last year, and I took on managing the Inn a couple weeks ago. With my grandparents taking a step back, it was my turn to step up, and I have a lot of ideas for the Brookrose.

The first? To get the Brookrose on the Colorado Rockies wedding circuit.

In my totally humble (read: biased) opinion, Mirror Valley is the *perfect* place to get married. Picture small town flair, gorgeous mountain backdrop, and a rustic Main Street. The town is attracting more and more tourists by the year, and we should capitalize on that.

Which is why I pitched (okay, begged) my brother to have his wedding here instead of at the courthouse. And after some gentle prodding, lots of puppy dog eyes, and from the goodness in his heart (along with the promise of my home-made snickerdoodles on request for the next five years), he acquiesced.

Hence, the partly selfish motivation to make sure this wedding goes off without a hitch.

The French doors open onto the Brookrose's gorgeous garden and my shoulders relax as I walk towards the gazebo. The warm spring air envelops my body, and the smell of blossoming flowers fills my lungs. There's a good chance I'll be sneezing my head off in a moment—gotta love allergy season—but for now, I want to enjoy this. Winters in Mirror Valley can be harsh, and the early summer is all the more sweet when it arrives.

I stop in front of the gazebo and feel a small bloom of pride. The midday sun is hitting *just* right, setting off the dark brown trim against the white columns. The branches of willow trees dangle just behind. This is where I always dreamed I'd have my own wedding. If I ever get married.

Which, honestly, seems even less likely right now than the *Real Housewives* not wearing fake tan. Unless they use Dorito cheese dust. I can almost imagine them sprinkling it on looking like the guy in that meme—sassy flair and all.

The thought almost makes me laugh uncontrollably.

Can you tell that I haven't eaten much today? I need to find snacks, ASAP.

"So, here's what I'm thinking," I say to extract myself from any more Dorito-related thoughts (except planning to grab Doritos when I have a minute). I hold up my clipboard, but I don't need my notes. "You two will stand there for the ceremony, and the chairs will stretch towards the creek on the far side. That way, no one will be blinded by the sun, and the photographer will have lots of space..."

Luke and Elly both nod along, but their eyes are glazed over. And for the thousandth time, I'm surprised to see it. When I took on a bigger role with wedding planning, I was ready for Elly to be your hyper-involved, super-detail-specific type. So, I over-prepared, made sure I had notes on every little thing. I guess I expected her to be...

Well, I won't say bridezilla. That's rude.

But surely, you'd think weddings are a trending topic on TikTok. I've even heard the word "Weddingtok" floating around amongst the happily-paired-ups in Mirror Valley.

Luke says that she's been too busy planning her bachelorette to really get involved with the wedding. Which is fair, I suppose. And it works for me—with my brother taking the lead, it means more time spent with him before he leaves.

Luke's that kind of guy anyway. He likes tradition, cares about doing things "the right way." Having a nice wedding matters to him, just like having a proper Fourth of July barbecue, or a roast turkey at Thanksgiving (and Luke Brooks does make the best roast turkey in all of Colorado). My brother believes that a wedding ceremony with all of his and Elly's loved ones will set the tone for their marriage.

It helps that he's got the money for it. His accounting job might bore me to hear about, but it sure does pay the bills and then some.

This is another point that sets Luke and me apart—where he's a successful CPA with a fiancée and a 401K, I'm a newly-graduated hotel manager who's been single about as long as my house spider, Gary. Though I have noticed Gary getting rather friendly lately with the ladybug who visits my orchids...

Yes, this is my life. Eternal plant and bug mom over here.

The irony is not lost on me that the forever-single girl is planning this wedding. A wedding where I don't even have a date.

After we finish at the gazebo, we walk back towards the

Inn. Luke and Elly didn't have much to contribute, but I take notes anyway.

"Let's take a break before the caterer gets here," Luke says. He and Elly are holding hands, and he gazes at her tenderly. "Babe, why don't you go inside and have some lunch? I need to talk to Ivy."

Elly crosses her arms, the flowing fabric of her boho dress shifting with the movement. "Don't take too long, Lukey. You know I hate eating alone."

I fiddle with my notes to give them privacy while they kiss, then Elly floats off inside the Inn. Luke's cheeks are slightly flushed and he's got a sweet grin on his face as he watches her. My heart softens for him. Elly might annoy me sometimes, but I could never fault her for how happy she makes my brother.

"You two are very sweet," I say sincerely. "I'm happy for you."

"Thanks," he says. Then, his expression changes. His smile turns sheepish as he runs his fingers through his dark blond hair. "Listen, I have to tell you something..."

My spine straightens. I'd recognize that tone anywhere —it's Luke's "I did something bad" voice, mixed with a hint of "please don't hate me."

"What did you do?" I grumble.

"Well." He shifts from foot to foot. Luke isn't a shifty person, so this immediately puts me on edge. "You know James?"

My heart slams against my ribcage. "James? James who?" I ask, even though I'm pretty sure I know the answer.

"James Weston."

Ugh. He had to go and say it.

I know I asked, but still.

"Yes, I know James." My voice is clipped.

Luke is apparently fascinated by the bush just behind me. "And you know how he'll be in town for the wedding?"

My lips pinch together. "He's coming back to Mirror Valley?"

"Well, he's not going to miss my wedding, is he?" Luke gives me a look. "But what I haven't had a chance to tell you yet is he's not just coming back to town. He's coming to the Brookrose."

"Come again?"

"He's staying here. In one of the guest rooms I booked for the wedding."

"I thought you booked those for the out-of-towners."

"Well, if we want to get nitpicky," Luke says. "*Technically*, he is from out of town."

"His parents live here."

"He doesn't. He lives in Denver. *And*," Luke adds, his voice taking on that same logical, matter-of-fact quality as when he talks about numbers. "He's actually the most out-of-town guest we have, seeing as he was born in England."

"And moved here when he was seven."

"It counts."

I guess... If we're going on *technicalities*.

Mr. and Mrs. Weston are warm, lovely people, and when I was younger and particularly obsessed with British culture, I used to spend hours soaking up their accents and mannerisms. They're an integral part of the Mirror Valley community now, all the more because they introduced our town to Yorkshire pudding and Banoffee pie (trust me, there's no going back to a Banoffee-pie-less existence).

I often wondered how someone like James could be their child. Even his younger twin brothers—Jake and Jesse —are your cream-of-the-crop gentlemen.

James is more of your anti-prince-charming—not quite

the villain, but he'd probably drop you on purpose if you were dancing together at the royal ball.

"This can't *really* be a surprise, can it?" my brother asks now. "James is one of my best friends. Of course I'd want him staying here for the wedding."

No, it isn't a surprise. In fact, I think a part of me has been waiting for this. I've gone out of my way over the years to avoid any James-related topics of conversation, tuned out whenever my brother spoke about him. I should've expected this, but I did the ostrich thing and buried my head in the sand.

The good news is that the wedding isn't for another couple weeks, which means that I have time to prepare myself. When I see him again, I'll be the epitome of "cool as a cucumber." No, something even cooler than that—cool as one of those dragon fruit things. Those are cool, right?

I'm pretty out of touch with anything deemed "trendy" or "on fleek" by kids these days. But if I was a fruit, I think I'd want to be a dragon fruit. Bright pink exterior hiding a speckled black-and-white inside. Plus, the name is *fierce*.

Shut up, brain.

"It makes sense," I finally manage, exhaling a full breath. "And I promise to play nice. This is your wedding, and I want you to be happy, first and foremost."

"Thank you," Luke says, placing a hand on my wrist. "That means a lot to me, Iv. I know how hard this is going to be for you."

I shoot him a look at his teasing tone, and stick my tongue out at him. We might be adults now, but that doesn't mean we don't occasionally give each other a hard time like we're thirteen again. Luke smiles that rare, bright smile of his.

"This isn't about me," I say, tapping my clipboard with finality. "This is about you and the future Mrs. Wilkes-

Brooks. We're going to make this the best wedding you could ask for."

"If anyone can put together a dream wedding on short notice, it's you."

He throws an arm over my shoulder as we head back inside. I peek up at my older brother, wondering if he, too, is thinking about our parents and what it'd be like to have them here with us. Big celebrations like this are always bittersweet.

But Luke's expression is neutral, stable. Just like he is. Just like he had to be.

We reach the front desk and I decide to check on a few things for the Inn before the caterer arrives. The Doritos will have to wait, there's just too much to be done.

Luke makes to go to the dining room, then stops mid-step. "Oh, Iv? There's one more thing."

"What's that?"

"You know how the wedding's happening next Saturday?"

"Of course."

"Well, James is arriving a little earlier than the other guests..."

I look up at him, narrow my eyes. "Early like?"

Luke checks his watch. "Early like now."

My jaw drops, but before I can say a word, Luke is gone. Disappeared into the dining room. Leaving me alone, exposed and vulnerable for whenever James Weston strolls in.

CHAPTER TWO

IVY

I take a long swig of my now-cold coffee, my heart banging out an irregular rhythm.

James Weston is coming here. He's staying at the Brookrose.

Okay, Ivy. It's cool.

Deep breath in, deep breath out. Just like in yoga.

I try to listen to myself, but my mind is already fifteen steps ahead. Breathing isn't nearly as important as damage control.

I flip open the Inn's ancient reservation book—I plan to bring us to the digital age ASAP—and scan through the bookings. Though the wedding is happening next Saturday, Luke's booked out blocks of rooms according to how close he and Elly are with the guests. We have a handful of people arriving this weekend and through next week. This week, we have...

Yes. There is one room booked starting today. With Luke's neat and tidy signature on it. Too tidy, too innocent.

The traitor.

At that moment, the door to the Inn opens, shocking me so bad that my arm jerks and my coffee sloshes upwards. I let out a squawk as the cold liquid drops back on me, staining the front of my white lace blouse.

"No!" I squeak, looking up to see whether the newcomer saw my blunder.

I'm even more mortified when I see that it's none other than Cam Harris—the founder of our town's top cleaning company, and the guy that I've been crushing on for months.

So I do what any smart, reasonable, rational woman would do when she sees her crush and has coffee spilled down her shirt...

I dive behind the front desk.

All thoughts of James Weston are temporarily forgotten as I curl into a ball and pray that Valentina—our capable and wonderful receptionist—comes back from her break soon. Preferably with more coffee that her husband, Ethan, brewed up at his cafe.

Not that coffee matters right now. This is crisis mode X100.

I cross all my fingers, cross my arms, squeeze my eyes shut, and pray that Cam didn't see me.

I hear his footsteps wander through the lobby and I scramble for my phone in my back pocket. Dial the only person on earth who might be able to help me.

"Daisy!" I whisper-shout when my best friend finally picks up.

"Yes. Who is this?" I hear her frown through the phone. "If you're looking to sell me one of those fancy vacuums, I've already got one, thanks."

"No, it's me!"

"Ivy? What's wrong with your voice?"

"Long story. Listen, are you at work?"

"Just finished. Why?"

"Any chance you can pop by the Inn? Cam's just walked in and—"

"Oooooh, Cam," Daisy sings. "Ivy and Cam. You two would have the sweetest couple name. Ivam."

I wince despite myself. There must be something better than *Ivam*.

Cavy?

Nope, that's not great either. Sigh.

"Do you happen to have an extra shirt at the gym?" I say quickly. "I just spilled coffee all over myself. I can't face him like this."

"Again? You need to get your limbs under control around him."

"Easier said than done," I grumble. "I'm cursed, remember?"

Daisy laughs, the sound bubbling through the phone. "You are *not* cursed."

"I am. When it comes to guys, I lose all motor coordination."

"And for those of us who failed biology...?"

"I flail around like a newborn giraffe, but not nearly as cute."

Daisy laughs again. "Ooh! Or one of those weird, tall bugs. Praying mantis."

I cringe, peek around the desk. Cam's at the other side of the lobby, staring at a generic landscape painting. "I'm so jealous of the girls in movies and books who make 'klutzy' look like an adorable character trait. There's always some dude who's ready to fall for a girl who trips and stumbles and knocks things over. Let me tell you, there's nothing cute about it when I'm klutzy."

"I have to agree with you there," Daisy says seriously and I'm not even mad. It's just the truth. "I'm sorry, Iv, but

I'm meeting my sister for a late lunch. Any way I can swing by after?"

I press my lips together. I knew it was a long shot. "That's okay, Dais. Yeah, drop by later, if you'd like." My lips turn down at the corners. "You'll never guess who's checking in toda—"

DING.

I sew my lips shut. Someone—probably Cam—rang the bell on the desk. He's standing, waiting for me.

"Everything okay?" Daisy asks.

Yoga breath in... out...

Oh, who am I kidding? How am I supposed to get out of this one?!

I glance one way, then the other. But there's no way around it.

I have to get up. I have to stand, face Cam, pretend that I wasn't cowering behind the desk, panic-dialing my best friend.

"Gotta go," I squeak.

Take another deep, yoga-rific breath in.

Shoot to a stand and come face-to-face with my crush.

"Hey, Cam," I say in what I hope is a confident, blasé sort of voice.

He looks even cuter close up with his slicked-back blond hair, round brown eyes, and cheek dimples. Most people say that Cam has a baby face, but I don't understand how that could possibly be a bad thing. He dresses so well too, wearing slacks and a dressy blazer no matter the weather. It makes my coffee-stained shirt all the more humiliating.

He cocks an eyebrow, his dark eyes skating from my hair —tied into a limp ponytail—down to the offensive stain. He has the grace to meet my eyes again, and I suddenly have a very real fear that my glasses are horribly lopsided or something. It'd be just my luck.

Luckily, his lips form that adorable grin of his. "Enjoyed your coffee?"

I hesitate for a fraction of a second and then laugh a little too loudly. I gesture down at my shirt, knocking the top of the desk by accident with my knuckles. "Enjoyed *wearing* it."

Ugh. Why am I laughing like a hyena at my own joke?

To my gratification, Cam chuckles. A loud—slightly short, but still nice—chuckle. He fiddles with the cuffs of his navy button-up shirt before placing his hands on the desk and leaning forward.

I have to take an instinctive step back as he towers over me. Cam is very tall and very slim. Some people call him lanky, but I'd say that—if you watched the *Twilight* movies as secretly-religiously as I did in high school—his physique is more akin to Edward than Jacob. He's too busy running his business to run on a treadmill, and I respect that.

"You're funny," he says.

Well, at least I have that going for me.

I tilt my chin up, crossing my arms in an attempt to hide the stain while also appearing cute. Unfortunately, the stain is lower than anticipated, so I end up curling over, caving in my chest so I'm looking at him at an unnatural angle.

Hunchback of Notre Dame is sexy, right?

"So, uh..." I clear my throat. "What can I do for you?"

"I'm here to check our new trainee's work."

"Right!" I say, work-Ivy coming back on shift. I release my hunchback pose and finger through the notes I took while talking to Grams this morning. "Dylan's cleaning Room 11, he should be finishing up soon."

"Great. I'll give him a hand if he needs it." Cam nods and I fall a little more for that can-do attitude of his.

I reach behind the desk for the key. "Room 11 is upstairs and to the right. Check-in's not until 4pm, so there's time."

"No problem. At Clear Reflections, we don't do customer satisfaction, we do customer delight." He grins, all dimples, looking proud as can be. "We'll get it done... Even if it takes all night."

The way he says this, the way he's staring right into my eyes, makes a weird feeling rise up through my body. I stutter over my words. "Well, actually, it can't take all night. Someone's checking in later and all that..."

I trail off into nothing as Cam's smile grows. "I'll give you an update soon. We could talk about it just the two of us. Maybe over a drink at McGarry's."

Oh.

OH!

My extremely slow brain finally clues in and my mouth drops open. "A drink? Wi—with me?"

Cam nods. "Unless there's another cute front desk girl I can ask."

Okay, so *technically* I'm the manager now. But I wouldn't expect Cam to just remember my promotion. He's only ever dealt with my grandparents as the managers—they're the ones who signed the contract with his cleaning company.

And yes, I want to meet him for a drink, but I'm rusty at this whole "say yes to the date" business (though *Say Yes to the Dress* is one of my favorite TV shows, when I have time to watch it). I'm assuming the crying and laughing and snotting and resounding "yes" thing is a no-go for dating?

I keep my smile flirty, stand with my hip jutted out. I go to place my hand on the desk oh-so-cutely. "I could be talked into i—"

182

My hand lands on the reservation book, which then falls to the floor under my weight.

Suddenly, I'm plunging sideways through the air, and I stumble. My hip bumps into the wall behind me, sending pain radiating down my leg. "Oof!"

Luckily, I manage to regain my balance before I'm flopped unceremoniously onto the floor with the rest of my dignity.

I wince as I rub my sore hip. My cheeks are burning when I finally bring myself to look at Cam.

His deep, round eyes are concerned. Though if it's for my injury or for my sanity, I can't tell. "You okay?" he asks.

I wave a hand, even as I subtly lift my leg to relieve some of the pressure on my hip. "I'm fine! Totally fine. I meant to do that."

Cam nods. "I better check on Dylan. See you later."

With that, he walks up the stairs, and I smile after him, still rubbing my hip.

As soon as he's out of sight, I turn away, cursing my un-adorable klutziness for the millionth time.

Cam Harris was trying to ask me out, wasn't he? And I had to go and put my hand where it didn't belong. Did I just ruin my one and only shot?

All of a sudden, there's a clap.

A slow, persistent clap, just behind me.

My heart sinks to my tiptoes and my stomach clenches into a ball. *For the love of all that is good and holy... Please, please don't let that be who I think it is.*

The clapping continues and I finally find the courage to turn around.

And there he is. The one person I hoped I'd never have to see again. My nemesis. The devil in disguise. My brother's best friend.

James *freaking* Weston.

CHAPTER THREE

JAMES

I'm staring. I know I'm staring.

I should stop... but I can't.

You know that feeling when you put something down and leave the room, but when you come back for it, it isn't there anymore? That's *kind of* close to where I'm at right now.

I'm not sure what I was expecting when I crossed paths with Ivy Brooks again. Apparently, my brain froze her in time, because I was picturing the blue jean capris, the colorful T-shirt with clashing patterns, the bright blue eyeshadow, and the braces. I imagined her slightly chubby apple cheeks, her wide, green eyes that were a little too big for her face.

And the bangs. I forgot about the bangs.

I'm surprised I haven't seen my best friend's little sister once in the past eight years. But when Luke told me that he was getting married, I knew I'd have to see her again.

On my one-a-day flight from Denver to the tiny Mirror Valley airport, I didn't think about it, threw myself into work. Mostly because I have a lot to get done, even while on "vacation." I actually went into the office this morning before my flight, and am still wearing my work clothes.

Which means that I am sticking out like a sore thumb.

Don't get me wrong, people in Mirror Valley wear suits... to weddings, funerals, and church on Sunday. My hometown is the kind of place for well-worn jeans with the bottoms frayed out, comfy flannel shirts, and baseball caps with faded logos. As much as I like wearing designer suits in the city, every time I come back—a rare occurrence, honestly—it's like my jeans somehow fit me better here.

So, when I walked into the Brookrose, all I was thinking about was changing into a Henley and my favorite blue jeans.

Until I saw the woman behind the front desk and stopped in my tracks.

I'd recognize her anywhere. Her chocolate brown hair is longer now, and tied in a messy ponytail so strands fall around her face. She's grown into her emerald eyes, still huge and wide behind Coke-bottle glasses. And her cheeks aren't as chubby, but her golden constellation of freckles are brighter than ever.

Is it just me or is she taller? Can women grow after they turn sixteen?

If anyone could do it, it's Ivy.

Thankfully, she doesn't see me staring—I would hear about it otherwise. She's too busy talking to the guy on the other side of the desk, waving her hands around as she speaks. I used to make fun of her for that, ask if she was conjuring spells or something.

I've since learned that moving your hands while talking is a sign of intelligence.

Yeah. That checks out.

Ivy giggles and runs her fingers through her ponytail, and I realize what's going on—she *likes* this guy.

A smile spreads across my lips as I watch the show; it would be rude to interrupt. I size him up—funny enough, he too is wearing a suit. Must be an out-of-towner.

As for Ivy, her flirting technique clearly hasn't changed since high school—lots of fidgeting, and playing with her hair, and laughing that sweet, light giggle that makes all eyes within a five-mile radius turn to her.

It's working—the guy's eating it up. I'm not surprised when he asks her out.

I'm also not surprised by her response—to keel over sideways into the wall.

Classic Ivy.

I can't help myself. I have to clap.

Who wouldn't clap for that?

Now, as she stares at me, shock written across her face, all I can think is that this is the last thing I could've expected. The cute, quirky teenage girl I went to school with has turned into this animated, beautiful woman. With a coffee stain in the shape of Australia on her blouse.

And really, this is the perfect way for Ivy and me to see each other again all these years later. After everything that's happened, everything we put each other through.

"Hey, Brooks," I say, and the name rolls off my tongue. Muscle memory. "Long time, no see."

CHAPTER FOUR
IVY

I stare at the mirage of a person in front of me for a long moment. Too long. Then, I open my mouth, unsure what exactly is going to come out.

"Jaaaaaaames!" I slather in this high falsetto I don't recognize. Guess we're going the kill-em-with-kindness route. "How are you, old bean?"

I've watched too many British films.

James leans back against the door and looks at me. Really looks at me. Trails those cool, blue-green eyes down my body in a way that makes me want to fidget and cover myself up. His eyes have to be one of his most disarming qualities—calm, still and unassuming as a tropical ocean, but with so many mysteries lurking beneath the surface. They might as well be MI6 agents, the both of them.

Shut up, brain.

"Good to see you," he says, and that deep voice resonates through my body.

There it is. The lilt of his faded English accent.

"Isn't it?" I say sweetly as I pick up the reservation book from the floor, plop it on the desk and throw it open, strictly business. I promised Luke that I would be nice, and I wouldn't break that promise. "You're wanting to check in?"

"Who was that?" James asks instead of answering my really very simple question.

"Who?" I blink, pushing my glasses up my nose.

"That guy who went upstairs." James's full lips twitch as he approaches. His stride is long and casual. "The man who I *think* you were trying to flirt with."

He sidles up to the desk, so close that I can almost smell what I'm sure is some overpowering musky cologne. I look up at him—how on earth is the guy so tall? Doesn't he have a castle atop a beanstalk to protect?

Okay, he's about the same height as Cam. But he's more muscular, so he just screams "fee-fi-fo-fum."

"I don't know what you're talking about," I say.

"Sure you do." James's eyes are still traveling over me, lazily exploring my face before meeting my gaze. The icy turquoise of his irises shoots right through me like daggers. "You were wriggling around like a drunk orangutan."

That's actually probably the most accurate description I've heard of my attempts at flirting.

I steel myself. I can be nice and still draw my line in the sand. "That's not any of your business."

James's lips quirk, his eyes still locked on mine. Something clenches deep in my stomach. "Guess you're right. It's not my business anymore."

There's a heavy, loaded silence as we glare at each other, and then I look away. I lay my finger on the reservation book and scan down until I see Luke's tidy signature again. "You're staying in one of our King rooms. Should be nice and spacious for all your jockstraps and soccer gear."

His eyes dance. "Don't you mean 'football' gear?"

My nostrils flare. Of course he would say that. There was a period in high school—at the peak of my Anglophilic phase—where I'd refuse to call it "soccer" and only referred to it as "football." Given that James was the top athlete on our high school soccer team, he liked to give me a hard time about it.

On top of everything else we argued about.

"I mean what I mean," I say flippantly. Like that makes any sense at all. I make a note on the reservation book. "You only reserved for one guest, so if you're bringing a lady friend, you'll have to pay extra."

"Nope, just me."

"Really." I stand straight, hands on my hips. "Going to the wedding solo? Couldn't find a date?"

James's lips twitch again, rather distractingly, although I'm too focused on gloating to pay much attention. "Something like that."

I can't help myself. I smile smugly. "Oh, James, don't you worry. You'll find a woman who's willing to put up with you someday."

He chuckles. "Does this mean you've got a date? Maybe BabyFace McGee over there?"

Yikes. I did not think this through. Because he's right, I don't have a date either, but I won't be telling him that. "What did I say about minding your business?"

Before James can respond, I turn on my heel and file through the keys, looking for Room 6. I take a moment to gather myself, catch my breath.

Slow down, this is James. You haven't seen each other in years, no need to fall back on old patterns. Be nice.

But why, oh why, didn't Luke tell me? I had no time to get ready. No time to take my hair down, put in my contacts, even change my shirt. No chance of throwing on that cool, confident glimmer and shine I always imagined I'd have when I saw James again.

Nope. Instead, he's seeing the girl in the movie before

the glamorous makeover. It's not that I care what he thinks, but I'm vulnerable in one too many places right now.

I sneak a glance over my shoulder.

Cowbells. He looks good.

His black hair's all grown-out and spiky in a way that looks like he's just woken up and run his fingers through it. He's gained muscle since the last time I saw him—especially in the upper body and arm regions. And though he's wearing nice slacks and a white dress shirt with the top button undone to show off a triangle of his firm chest, he looks right at home in our cozy country inn.

Though with that level of cockiness, he probably makes himself at home wherever he goes. Probably thinks he rightfully belongs on Her Majesty's throne.

The scoreboard is clear: James - 1, Ivy - 0.

"You know it's rude to stare, right?" he asks.

My cheeks flush a furious shade of red as I turn back to the keys. I fiddle some more, pretending I didn't hear him, then grab the right one. I throw the key at him. "There you go. Room 6 is just down the hall on the left."

"You're not going to show me to my room?"

"Surely, you can find it yourself. Or are you prone to getting lost in small spaces?"

"I was under the impression that the Brookrose was one of the top-rated hotels in the area for its hospitality." James tsks, shaking his head. "What a disappointment."

I press my lips together. Man, he drives me up the wall!

We haven't seen each other in years but he knows *exactly* which of my buttons to push. It's like he somehow senses how important it is to me that I run the Inn to perfection.

Letting out a small, frustrated breath, I sidle around the desk and gesture down the hallway with a deep bow. "Follow me, sir."

"I like when you call me that."

I shoot him another glare before turning on my heel and strutting away. James is light on his feet—probably all those stupid calf muscles—but he's behind me, keeping my pace.

"Number 6, huh?" I can hear him smirking. "Is that referring to something?"

I roll my eyes, though he can't see it. "What would it be referring to?"

"Well, I believe you were six when we first met. I wouldn't put it past you to give me this room as a way of declaring your everlasting love for me."

I almost gag. "Guh. Puke."

James chuckles. When he speaks again, his tone is conversational. "Are you excited for the wedding?"

"Luke and El—Lenore's wedding?" I say. "What do you think?"

"I think you're over the moon about it."

There's a serious note in James's voice that I can't quite work out. I look over my shoulder at him, but his face is the Switzerland of expressions, so I shrug. "I want Luke to be happy."

"I get that. I was pretty honored when he asked me to be his best man—Oof!"

James lets out a grunt as he runs into me, feinting sideways so as not to knock me over. Because my legs have stopped working. I'm frozen in the middle of the hallway, my heart leaping. "He did *what*?"

"Asked me to be his best man. You didn't know that?"

Freaking Luke!

"Yeah. Of course. I knew that," I find myself saying, even as I imagine the different ways I might lightly poison my brother with my next batch of snickerdoodles. A small dose of laxatives should do the trick.

"It's not a big deal." James shrugs. "I'll be helping with wedding errands so I won't be around much."

I sigh miserably. "I am also helping with wedding planning."

James's eyes widen a fraction. "Oh."

"So we'll be seeing a lot of each other."

"Looks like it."

"Great. Wonderful." My head bobs up and down. I gesture stiffly towards Room 6. "There you are. Go nuts."

"I will." James shoots me a dazzling smile. "I'll see you soon for the meeting with the caterer."

"Can't wait." I match his smile, holding up an overenthusiastic thumbs up. Then, I march back down the hallway, hoping that my stride hides the fact that I'm currently dying inside.

You know how I said that I felt it when things were wrong?

Well, James Weston definitely goes on the *wrong* list. And now, I have to spend the next couple of weeks pretending that I can get along with the guy. Pretending that he hadn't made it his personal life mission in high school to make me miserable.

Wonderful, indeed.

ALSO BY SARA JANE WOODLEY

Love in Mirror Valley

The Next Worst Thing

The Right Wrong Match

The Real Fake Fiancé

Aston Falls (sweet contemporary romance)

More Than Second Chances

More Than Just Friends

More Than Meets the Eye

Legacy Inn (sweet YA romance)

The Summer I Fell for My Best Friend

The Summer I Fell for My Fake Boyfriend

The Summer I Fell for a Billionaire

The Summer I Fell for My Enemy

Made in the USA
Las Vegas, NV
24 February 2023

68084094R00114